# COVER MY EYES

## TAYLOR BARRETT

Published in Canada by Engen Books, Chapel Arm, NL.

A CIP catalogue record for this book is available from Library and Archives Canada.

ISBN-13 (print): 978-1-77478-194-4

Distributed by:
Engen Books
www.engenbooks.com
submissions@engenbooks.com

First mass market paperback printing: June 2025

Cover Design: Ellen Curtis

# COVER MY EYES

## TAYLOR BARRETT

For Ms. Taylor and Ms. Rose.
I couldn't have done this without you!

# PREFACE
## KANSAS, OCTOBER 1931

### ELEANOR

"I lost my job."

Joseph sighed and nodded. Eleanor had known it was coming. They both had. She just hadn't realized how soon it would happen. From the look of it, Joseph wasn't surprised in the slightest.

"You're not getting it back, are you?" he asked. His voice was low and his eyes were dark as he stared down into his empty teacup.

Eleanor shook her head without saying "No, I'm not." Partially, this was because he didn't really need her to say it in order to know, but also because she didn't want to have to admit it.

Joseph pushed back his hair and said with a humorless laugh, "The man who owns the barn in town, Atticus Jones, is hiring an executioner. That's what I've heard, anyway. Maybe you could do that."

"No. Absolutely not," Eleanor set down her teacup and watched the ceiling's reflection on the yellowed inside. "After what happened with Hugh, I..."

"Don't worry about it, Eleanor. You'll be alright. You'll make some money somehow."

Eleanor was certain that Joseph knew that she cared more about her job itself than the money, but she nodded along anyway, brushing a curl away from her face and letting out a long breath as her shoulders sagged back against the wooden chair. It dug uncomfortably into her shoulders, and she frowned.

"You could always come stay with me. Or, actually, take Aunt Clara's cabin in Indiana. You do know that, don't you?"

She smiled at him. "I should be the one saying that, Joe. You shouldn't have to look after me. I'm your big sister."

"You've taken care of me for long enough. Maybe you deserve to be looked after every once in a while, too."

Eleanor stood and made her way to the kitchen sink where she set her teacup. "I appreciate that. I really do. But, I'll be alright. I just need another job."

Joseph's chair scraped the hardwood floor as he pushed it away from the table and came to meet her at the sink, leaning heavily on his cane. The sound of the chair reminded Eleanor of being at work with the kids who ran their fingernails across the chalkboard, and who laughed when she would wince and shake her head. She blinked and turned around.

Joseph's kitchen was homey. Homey, Eleanor thought, in a way that was much different than her own house or the school. The house was small, the kitchen being one of the smallest rooms in the house. There was a window over the oven with a view of the river out back and a steel sink in the corner of the room, where she stood and let her gaze stray to her brother.

"I did see this woman the other day, though," she told him. "She was at the market at the same time as I was. We went to the same bread vendor."

"Did this woman offer you a job?" Joseph asked, tipping his head back as he drained the rest of his tea and set the cup next to Eleanor's in the sink.

"No, but she was talking to the vendor, and he told her about a job at the market, selling tomatoes," Eleanor paused, ripping at a hangnail. "I should learn to garden."

Joseph huffed out a laugh, shaking his head

a little as he leaned back against the counter. "At least think about Atticus Jones, Eleanor. He could have something for you to do. I've heard that he has something for everybody."

## JAMIE

"My parents named me Jamie after my grandmother, and my grandmother was not a coward," Jamie told herself as she glared into the dusty, fingerprint-covered mirror. She shivered when her reflection glared back. "My grandmother was not poor, she was not unemployed, and she was not alone."

This hit Jamie very hard two days later, when she received an eviction notice on the morning of November thirteenth, 1931.

"What is this?" she asked the man who had handed her the slip of paper.

"An eviction notice," he said simply, peering at her in a bored manner with half-lidded eyes.

"Why?"

"Because your taxes have not been paid in five

months."

"But I will get them paid. I'm looking for a job now."

"Too bad," said the man with a wave of his hand, in a way Jamie wanted to pull his mustache hairs out one by one. "Come up with the money in thirty days, or you're out."

Jamie groaned and turned around, slamming the door behind her and kicking it, just for good measure. She crossed her arms and looked around. She wished there were somebody to tell her what to do.

The flyer on the kitchen table suddenly seemed very loud. *Executioner*. It was, Jamie thought, a big and bloody word, one that possibly came with big and bloody consequences. But, it could get her taxes paid.

"I'll do it," she muttered, picking up the flyer and tracing her fingers over the words. "Evicted… over my dead body."

# ONE
# NOVEMBER 1931

I meant it when I told him that I would do whatever it took to get the money. I think anybody would have.

I should have kept my mouth shut.

Now, I stood in a run down, wet-smelling barn with a man who was pacing back and forth and sizing me up. I was rather tall for my age, but I did not think that this was what he was observing. Instead, I think that he was questioning why he should hire a woman.

This was to be expected. Men liked to look at us women, especially ones who were alone, or ones who were below them, and stare at us as if we were creatures from another planet if we asked for employment. They liked to belittle us, narrowing us down to our sex and nothing more. How dare we wish to make money? How dare we succeed?

The man—Atticus Jones—took me to the back of the run-down barn and sighed heavily, taking a seat on a haystack and stroking his ginger beard in thought. I noticed a spider crawling up the wall behind him and winced.

"I will do *anything*," I said earnestly. I had to sell my case, and I knew it. There were easily much more experienced people, taller and stronger people, who needed the money just as much, maybe more than I did.

"Anything?" he asked, raising his eyebrows as he looked me up and down.

"Anything," I confirmed.

He gave a little *hmph*.

"I swear, I'll do it. I will do whatever you need me to do."

An old, mousy brown horse stood up slowly and shook its head noisily before making its way to where Atticus was sitting. He laid a hand on its head and scratched between its ears. A housefly landed on the wall next to my shoulder, patiently awaiting Atticus' decision with me.

"You know, it's a tough job. Not just anybody can do it. I want to know for certain that you won't back out on me."

The horse snorted and snapped its teeth at Atticus, who tapped it lightly on the muzzle. I folded my arms across my chest and planted my feet.

"Mr. Jones, I *need* the money. I can handle it. There aren't too many people jumping at the chance to do this, are there?" I knew that wasn't exactly true, that I was lying through my teeth just to get the job, and I hated myself a bit for it. Anybody would have taken the job. Everybody was low on money. "I was a woodcutter for two years, so I know how to work with blades. I've taken meat-cutting classes and dealt with the cleanup, the blood, and the guts. I know that I can do this, too."

He was quiet, and for a moment, the only sounds were the horse's heavy breathing and the rustling of the trees outside. I pulled my coat tighter around my shoulders.

"Why should I give you the job?" he asked, one hand pausing on his chin.

"What do you mean?"

"Well, there are certainly men out there who would do this for me. Why should I bother giving the job to Little Red Riding Hood instead?"

I scoffed and unfolded my arms, planting them on my hips instead. "Do those men know how to cut through muscle? Could they keep a straight face when they cut it? Tell me the name of a man who has not once cut himself while cutting down trees, or burned himself while lighting a fire. Go on, Jones. Tell me."

Atticus kept his mouth closed, looking at me in an unimpressed manner. My stomach squirmed in worry.

"I'm alright with people, too," I went on, setting my jaw. "Most people, anyways. I know how to talk people down from things. I was the one who cared for my grandmother when she finally lost it. There are many reasons to hire me instead of one of those men who just want to hold a fancy sword."

He watched me carefully when I'd finished speaking, eyes trailing up and down my body.

"The pay is nice," he said finally. "You would have to start immediately, though. Tomorrow, seven o'clock in the evening."

"Thank you," I sighed. A weight slid from my chest to my feet and melted into the rotting wooden floorboards of the barn.

He leaned back against the hay and grinned, though not exactly happily, slapping his knee as he let out a loud whoop.

"We've got an executioner!"

"Thank you, Mr. Jones. Really."

Atticus clapped me on the shoulder with a warm, heavy hand. I winced. He was a large man with large hands and muscles, and I suddenly wondered why he didn't just do the executions himself.

"Go home. I'll see you tomorrow evening."

I shook his hand and tipped my head, but just as quickly as my relief had come, a feeling of immense dread had taken over, worming its way into my chest and sliding down to my stomach.

I had imagined myself doing many things in my life. As a girl, I had imagined being a princess or a chef. I had imagined myself, once my parents died, living the rest of my life with my grandmother. I had even seen myself, though quite vaguely, lovelessly marrying a man with too much money for his own good, probably an alcoholic, a tall man who would cheat on me on his way home from work, and taking his money while he was out, fleeing the state while he smoked a pipe with another woman.

I had never imagined myself as an executioner.

\*\*\*

I left the barn and went straight to the market to buy a loaf of bread. The sun was just setting, wrapping itself in the arms of the heavy November clouds and high winds. There was a rusty red truck parked on the side of the road near the market, one wheel removed, but nobody was nearby to fix it. The air smelled like herbs and flour, and there were, as always, too many sounds to pick out exactly what anybody was saying and who they were speaking to. People working at the stands often liked to poke their heads into the conversations of others, adding a little, "Isn't that the way it is," or "He'll be home soon, I bet." Though the crowds had died down in the last year, particularly in the last few months, the shrinking of the crowds was not all that signficant. The noise never stopped. It only seemed to get louder.

I stepped around a group of teenage boys in suspenders and flat hats who were standing in a circle, tossing a coin and chattering, and made my way to the bread vendor named Peter whom I had taken painting classes with when I was younger. He was a brown-skinned man with a thick black mustache and long, curly hair, and he liked to wear deep blues and emerald greens.

"Hello, Jamie. What's new?" he leaned against a wooden stand with his elbows and dropped his chin into his palm.

"I just got a job, that's what's new," I said. I picked up a loaf of bread, examined it carefully for any signs of mold, and dropped it in front of him.

"Really?" his eyebrows shot up and disappeared under his hair. "Did you speak with Mr.

Miller about selling your tomatoes?"

I shook my head and leaned in to say quietly, "I'm going to be an executioner."

He laughed, so loud and sudden that the man who was selling spices turned sharply to look, wide-eyed, at him. Still chuckling, he put out his hand to take the money I owed him.

"What?" I said, digging through my coin purse and handing him the money.

"Jamie, we don't do executions around here," his eyes were sincere, and his voice was tainted with something resembling pity, "let alone one performed by a woman."

"I'm sure that they have been," I shot back, grabbing my bread.

"Probably not for years, though. Hundreds, even." Peter looked around me to make sure that we weren't holding up a line. "Are you certain this is a real job that you've got? How much are they paying you?"

"More than I'd be earning by selling tomatoes with you, that's for sure," I said with a huff. "Jones thought that I was qualified, and I needed the money, alright? Isn't that enough?"

Peter sighed, held out both of his hands and waited for me to place mine in his. He folded his fingers around mine, watching my face intently.

"Be careful. I mean it. There's a lot that comes with this sort of job, I would imagine," he shook his head, squeezing my hands. "I wish you would just sell tomatoes like anybody else."

"I know you do," I retracted my hands and laid one on his shoulder. "But, I'm not anybody else. I'll live. I promise."

"Yes, yes, alright."

I waved goodbye and picked up my bread, beginning to walk off into a flurry of people who were crowded around a potato vendor. I shouted over my shoulder, "Have a nice evening!"

"You too, Jamie!" he called, one hand raised and one still resting against the table.

I shoved through the line around a woman selling apples, murmuring an occasional, "I'm sorry," and "Excuse me!" until I had gotten out and was breathing normally once again. The truck, I noticed, was still parked on the side of the road.

***

The night was heavy and cold, the air in the house hanging over me like a curtain. I ate my bread and tomato soup in silence, staring at the yellowed wallpaper in the kitchen. The corner of the table, I noticed that night, was chipped rather harshly, and there was a crack running down the wall by the stove, which was rusted past the point of fixing. Tucking that information into a pocket of my brain where I had decided I would store everything for when I got paid, I finished my supper and went to the bathroom, brushing my shoulder against the doorframe and wincing when I stepped on a creaky floorboard. There were more than a few boards in the bathroom that desperately needed to be fixed, ones that I hadn't gotten around to noticing until a few weeks ago. After staring into the mirror for a moment, I picked up my hairbrush and did my hair in the dark.

At ten o'clock, I lit a candle and got into bed. The frame made a low whine when I sat down. I ignored the howl of the coyotes outside as best as I could and pulled my sheets back, opening my book and shutting it again as I lay down and rolled onto my side.

I stared into the flame of the candle and thought for a while, mostly about the day that was to come. When I was fifteen, I took a butchering class with my grandmother, who had been a butcher herself when she was young. I hated every minute of it, waking up in the middle of the night with dreams of blood and knives. Maybe I had just been sensitive, but the blood had bothered me as a teenager. Then, I worked as a wood-cutter for two years, when I was seventeen and eighteen, and though I had enjoyed it, realized then that I didn't particularly want to work with an axe. Any person with an ounce of intelligence could see that being an executioner was not meant for me. Even I, who had begged for the job, regretted it a bit.

Now, I was about to work with a blade again, for the first time in almost five years. I wondered if my grandmother was proud of me.

I wondered if I was proud of myself, too.

## TWO

The realization was hot and sudden, like a knife that had been lying next to a burner for far too long had been shoved through my gut.

Today, I would be the reason that somebody died.

"Is there not a face covering?" I asked as Atticus held up the robes when we met before lunch.

"Why would you need a face covering?"

"So that people don't see my face. People aren't going to be happy about this, and I would much rather not be hunted."

"Don't worry about that. You'll be alright."

Atticus retrieved the sword, which he had been keeping in his farmhouse's basement for the last month or two. The sword was blunt and curved at the tip and had a gold handle with intricate detailings on it. He seemed ecstatic to finally be able to show it off to somebody, to finally have a use for it. I did not blame him—I knew that he must have spent a fortune on it. He handed it to me, eyeing me carefully as if to say, *don't you dare drop it.*

I did not drop it, but I did shiver at the cold metal in my palms, and I tried to picture myself in front of a swarm of people, holding it with confidence, but I couldn't seem to put my face into that picture.

"Who?" I asked.

He made a confused noise.

"Who am I executing?"

"Oh!" his brows drew together suddenly, and his hand came up to stroke his beard. "A woman named… Mary. Mary… uh… Mary Bell. Yes, that's it."

It struck me then that I had seen her name in the newspaper yesterday, though I hadn't yet read it.

"What did she do?"

"She killed her husband. Put a knife right through his chest and turned herself in." His voice was incredulous, and he shook his head as he spoke.

"Why?"

He shrugged. We were both quiet for a moment, and I handed him back the sword.

"Well, go have some lunch and be back here at seven o'clock. The execution will happen behind the barn."

I wondered briefly if this was even legal, whether Atticus was allowed to have this sword, where he got it, whether this thing that he was doing behind his family's barn had just been an idea that became a reality when somebody desperate enough showed up and executed the first person who had been turned in.

"Do you promise that you can do this?" he asked me on my way out. I spun around.

"What happens if I don't?"

"You don't get paid. Seems like a simple choice to me."

I said yes because I would have done whatever it took to get the money. I think that anybody would have.

\*\*\*

I heated my leftover tomato soup for lunch and watched the cornfield tremble through the window, the birds taking their share of it while I ate. The sun had come out from behind the clouds, a rare sight lately, but the wind had picked up, so much so that I had to close the windows before the house grew too cold.

A crow was sitting close to the window and watching me carefully. It seemed less like a crow and more like a taunting bully by the second. I was reminded of being in church as a child, feeling incredibly watched by God as I knelt in the pews and begged Him to forgive me, to tell me what I had done wrong. I felt like I had at my mother's and father's funeral, being eyed up and down, touched carefully on the shoulder, not like a china plate, but like a bomb, and stared up at by my younger cousins who could not fathom that my parents had drowned, that they were gone forever.

Struck with a sudden sense of deep unease, with the crow's eyes still locked on me, I rose from the kitchen table and poured the remaining soup down the sink, watching it pool and sputter at the drain's mouth until it ran down its esophagus, before rinsing the sink.

"Go. Away," I told the crow through a clenched jaw, but it did nothing but cock its head to the side like a child. Breathing heavily, I threw the moth-eaten curtain across the kitchen window with a bang and stalked off to my bedroom.

In the bedroom, I pulled on a long-sleeved black blouse and charcoal-colored trousers. I looked into the mirror, noticed that my lips looked pale, and pulled a pot of red lip stain from the cabinet above the sink. My face still looked odd, eyes circled in black and purple rings, the way they had been since I was eight years old, and bangs stuck to my forehead with cold sweat.

I wondered how I would look after the execution. Would my hands turn red? Would my cheeks cave in, eyes turn perpetually bloodshot? Partially, I wished that they would, so that I would not get out of this unscathed while a woman's head rolled down the dirt pathway of a family's farmhouse.

I should not, I later realized, have wished at all.

*** 

An hour before the execution, I stopped by the market to see Peter. He was lining up his loaves of bread in a neat row, after they had been jostled around by customers.

"Hi, Jamie," he greeted when he noticed me.

"Peter," I toyed with the stalk of a pepper on the table next to his, avoiding his eyes. "Have you heard anything about Mary Bell?"

"Oh, yes," he sighed, shaking his head. "I suppose you'll be performing her execution."

"That's what I wanted to ask you about. I asked Mr. Jones about why she's being executed, but he didn't say much. Do you know what she did?"

"It's all in yesterday's paper. They're saying that she killed her husband after finding out he had been having an affair."

"Really?" I breathed out, shocked.

"Really," he confirmed, leaning in close. "Apparently, he left Mary at home with their newborn son while he went to work, only for the other woman, Mrs. Adams, to visit Mary, telling her what had been happening. Mary was doubtful, but the husband admitted to it when she asked him. They'd been seeing each other for months, and now Mrs. Adams is pregnant."

"Is Mary's husband the father?"

"Of course he is. Mary got so angry that she drove a steak knife through his chest and left him on the floor to die. Then, she drove her son to her sister's house, and went to the sheriff to turn herself in."

I stared at him, blinking silently for a moment. "Are you sure?"

"That's what the paper said. Do you have a copy?"

"I do, but..." I looked down, picking at my cuticles. "Wow."

"Wow," Peter agreed. "So, when is the execution?"

***

The robes were a lot heavier than they looked. Or perhaps that was the impending guilt sitting like rocks in my pockets. In the crowd of people gathered behind the barn, I saw Peter and then saw a woman with long blonde curls and the prettiest face I had ever seen. To my horror, I also saw my littlest cousin, Addy, wearing a yellow bonnet and clutching the arm of my aunt Helen, whom I hadn't spoken to since my parents' funeral.

Atticus was speaking, his voice loud and clear over the low murmur of the crowd, a young woman with tied hands standing at his side. She was slim and tall, redheaded, and wearing an ankle-length navy blue dress with flowers on it. This was Mary Bell.

"May God have mercy upon your soul," he finished, and nodded to me. I took a step up onto a tall block of concrete, catching the bottom of my robes in the toe of my shoe and shaking off my foot discreetly. Mary sank to her knees willingly, laying her cheek against the wooden block with a gracefulness I could never have expected. I wanted to ask her why she did it, why she turned herself in, if her family was in the crowd, but she had yet to say a word, and she did not meet my eyes. And could I blame her?

I bent down to her level and whispered, "I'm sorry."

"I did this, and I knew that there would be consequences when I did," she said, unflinching.

"Forgive me."

She nodded once and reached out her hand for me to take like a mother reaching out to her child as they crossed the road. I clasped it with one hand and adjusted the sword so that it was more secure in my one-handed grip.

Closing my eyes, I raised my arm, sword in hand, and let it fall, waiting to hear the *thump* as it landed on the block. I had imagined how it would feel and how the onlookers would shriek, but nobody screamed except what sounded like a crowd of women toward the back. I opened my eyes, every ounce of my body protesting, to see that, oddly, hauntingly unaffected, people were watching me in awe, a twisted sort of fascination in their eyes and flowing from their open mouths.

I glanced down to see Mary's limp body lying in front of the block, which was now stained red, and her head on the other side of the block. I dropped her hand, letting it fall to her side. Halves of bones stuck out from her neck, blood dripping from wherever it could find an opening. My sword was dripping, too, but my hands were clean.

Momentarily, I stood frozen in place, breathing heavily over the deceased body of a woman I didn't even know, before Atticus marched up to the concrete block and shoved me back toward the barn, taking my sword with him and sheathing it as he went.

"Have a drink," he told me as his wife handed him a glass jar of water. I shook my head.

"I'm alright."

He watched as I took a slow seat on the wooden floor. I could hear the crowd dying away and heard them making their way back to their houses. The sun had now set, and the barn was cold and damp and smelled like grass and horses, and faintly like the metallic stench of blood.

"You're walking home?" Atticus grunted as he set the sword against the wall in the corner of the barn. I nodded.

"Be careful. People will be angry about this. Somebody might come looking for you."

The tips of my ears burned, and I clenched my hands into fists. Had he not been listening to what I had said earlier?

"Maybe, if I had covered my face—"

"It's too late," he said, shrugging. "They know who you are, now. If they wanted to find you badly enough, a face covering wouldn't stop anybody.

Besides, it's a small city. There are too many people, and they all look the same."

This was nowhere near as reassuring as I imagined he had thought it would be. It was quite the opposite. This was when I noticed that he was the kind of person who liked to hear himself speaking. It didn't matter if what he said had meaning, as long as he could say it.

"Thank you, Mr. Jones," I said, through gritted teeth.

"You were brave today, Jamie. Thank you. I've got your check in the house, just give me a moment to get it."

He left me on the floor, leaving the door unlocked behind him. Only then, sitting alone in the dark and the quiet, did it sink in that Mary Bell was really, truly dead, and that I was the reason.

## THREE

The check seemed heavy in my pocket on the walk home. Not only because, yes, the sum of money was large, and yes, the walk was rather long and taxing, but because the paper felt like it was caked with blood and made of lead and bone marrow. The whole time, I walked as if my feet were made of cement. What would my grandmother think? What would my parents think? I trudged along, eyes blurry and thighs stinging.

When I got inside, I locked the door, unlocked it, locked it again, and repeated the process twice more for good measure. Then, I went straight to my bedroom to grab yesterday's paper from my desk.

Mary Bell's photo was on the second page of the newspaper. I tore it out carefully, trying not to rip anything, and brought it with me to bed, holding it tightly enough that my fingers stained black as I got under the covers in my clothes.

"Did you really deserve to die?" I asked her photo, but she did not respond.

*Of course, she won't respond*, I chided myself, *you killed her*.

The paper confirmed what Peter had told me, nearly verbatim. Peter had always been a gossip, and I had hoped that he'd been exaggerating the details of the story. However, Mary Bell truly had killed her husband after finding out about his affair, and she had turned herself in for the murder.

I stared at the photo for so long that when I tore my eyes away and looked up at the ceiling where the paint was flaking and peeling, I could still see her delicate face, her wide eyes and full lips, button nose, and red ringlets.

"I'm sorry," I said finally, still looking at the ceiling. I tried to imagine her voice, but it didn't sound right in my ears, in the quiet of the room.

"I'm sorry," I repeated, a bit louder this time. My eyes were growing wet. I set Mary's photo down on the sheets beside me and rolled over to face it. "I really am sorry."

And still, as my eyes fell shut and the moon rose, big and white and full, I couldn't decide whether she might have forgiven me or not.

## FOUR

When I woke the next morning, back sore and head aching, I opened the drawer on my night-stand and tucked Mary's photo at the back behind my diary and matches. I tried not to think about it while I made myself a bowl of porridge and topped it with cinnamon, pushed it to the back of my mind while I pulled an apple from the tree outside, and laid the slices on top of my porridge. While I ate, I tried desperately to think of anything other than the night before.

The crows were out again, nibbling at my plants in the garden. Years ago, my grandmother and I had made a scarecrow to put in the cornfield, hoping to scare away the birds. Now, though, it did nothing to frighten them, and the crows seemed to have grown used to it and might even have begun to see it as a friend.

When I finished eating, I pulled on a purple blouse and dark brown pants and laced up my shoes on the way outside. Almost automatically, I started down the dirt road to the barn, where I passed a family of frogs who were croaking noisily, their ribbits low and strangled. They continued to croak until I got too close, then quieted at once, like children caught stealing bubblegum from a corner store, and darted behind a pile of rotting wood, moldy from moisture in the fog and morning condensation.

The sky only seemed to grow greyer the further I walked. The clouds were heavy around the barn, coating the sky in a dark, damp wash resembling watered-down oil paints. The land around the barn was also strikingly quiet that morning. It felt as if that was the only thing that had changed around the barn since the night before—a newfound silence. Atticus, surprisingly, was nowhere to be found. The usual sounds of whirring chainsaws and booming shouts and shrill talk from his wife, who watched him through the farmhouse's kitchen window, were all gone and had been replaced with a soft scrubbing noise, one so faint I nearly wondered if I had imagined it.

"Mr. Jones?" I called as I stepped into the barn.

I paused in the doorway, breath catching in my throat when I realized that it was not Atticus in the barn, but the lady who I had seen in last night's crowd, the one with the wide eyes and blonde hair. She stood near the far right corner of the barn, holding my sword in one hand and a sponge in the other. She had a wooden basin filled with cleaning supplies balanced on the window ledge behind her and a rusty metal bucket of water on the floor, and was dressed nicely, far too nicely, for somebody who was scrubbing old blood off of an executioner's sword, wearing a long-sleeved pink blouse and a long black skirt.

"He's not here, love," she said. Her voice was lyrical, with an accent that sounded close to English, but not quite. She set down her sponge and turned to face me, her eyes trailing from my shoes to my face, and settling on my eyes, which she held determinedly. "He's out getting bread."

"What are you doing?" I asked.

"Cleaning your sword. It's a bit gross, to be honest," she told me, holding up the sponge to show off the blood. I wrinkled my nose in disgust and she nodded approvingly.

"Are you working for Atticus, too?" I took a seat on a haystack near her. She shrugged lightly, setting the sword on the floor and coming to stand closer, back against the wall, and legs thrust out so that I could see her brown shoes and frilly white socks.

"I suppose so. He pays me, anyway. I needed some extra money, so when I found out about your whole... thing... I offered to clean your equipment and clean up behind the barn after the executions."

I thought momentarily about the way she had said *thing*. Not like she was disgusted, but more in a tone that suggested that she was curious, that she knew how it felt to be desperate for something, to be willing to do anything to get what you need.

"Thank you. I would probably hate to do an execution with somebody else's blood still on the sword." I wasn't sure if this was the right thing to say, but what else was there?

She smiled softly, but her eyes were questioning as she took a step toward me, hands behind her back, swinging one foot in front of the other.

"My name is Jamie, by the way," I said.

"I know," she nodded. "Jamie Foster. Kansas' one and only executioner. Atticus told me."

"Yes," I grimaced, "though I'd rather not be known just for that."

She tilted her head to the side a bit and said, "I'm Eleanor."

"Eleanor what?"

"Eleanor Collins." She didn't hesitate, didn't miss a beat, eyes peering into mine, peeling back my irises, and gazing into my brain. Hers were a deep, dark brown, the color of black coffee and dark chocolate, and her nose and cheeks were rosy from the cold. Her nose, I noticed, when she turned for a moment to glance out the window, had a bump on the bridge, where freckles were lightly splashed. It struck me that I might not have seen a prettier face in my life.

"Why did you come to watch the execution?" I asked, tearing my eyes away. Her blonde brows furrowed, and her lips pursed in an act that seemed involuntary.

"I was curious. I knew a little bit about the job, but I wasn't entirely convinced that the execution would really happen, to be honest. Part of me felt like Atticus would call it off," she bit her lip. "But he didn't. You know that already, though."

I shook my head. "I feel bad about it. I really do. That's why I came here. I need to speak with Atticus about it."

"I saw one of the little girls who I used to teach last night. Her name was Marie. She must have come with her grandparents to watch it happen, but she was so little, probably only ten years old now. I taught her when she was seven. I felt bad… she shouldn't have seen it happen. Not that young. I know Mary was not a criminal without a cause," she paused. "Mary wouldn't have done something like that unless that man who she married had hurt her badly enough."

I looked at my feet and heard Eleanor sigh heavily.

"That's why she killed him, actually," I said, assuming she hadn't read the newspaper yet. "He was having an affair."

She nodded slowly and looked up at the ceiling.

"Did you know her?" I asked.

"Not exactly. We used to teach at the same school, and we were never very close, but I know her well enough to know that she wouldn't have just killed somebody. It goes like this much too often, nowadays. Men drive women crazy and then they're the ones who lock them up. They made them like it, though."

I considered this for a moment. It was true, I thought, but I desperately wanted to get away from the subject at hand.

"Are you still a teacher?" I asked. It was a reasonable question since she did know all about my profession anyway. I would have liked to learn a bit more about hers.

"No," she said sadly. "The school where I used to teach, Pine Hill Elementary, closed last year. I've been nannying since, though, but it's been hard to find people who are looking for nannies recently."

"Why did you want to be a teacher? Did you like it?"

"Are you going to hammer me with questions for the rest of the day?" she laughed, throwing her head back just a little. Her teeth were very pretty, too, I noticed. She had a small gap between the front two.

"If you're willing to answer, then yes," I grinned, cheeks heating up.

Eleanor got a little closer. "I loved it. I just love children. My brother and I grew up rather isolated, and I took care of him often. I think that I just knew, because of how much I love him, that I would like to be there for other children in the same way that I always tried to be there for him. I knew that I wanted to do that forever."

I wanted to ask about her brother, about the rest of her life, but I didn't want to pry.

As if she had been sensing my curiosity, Eleanor said, "My childhood is too much to unload onto you right now. We can save that for another day."

*When?* When would I see her again?

Her eyes met mine again. She sat down on the floor in front of me, holding out her hands, keeping her gaze on my face as I slotted my hands into hers and let her intertwine our fingers.

"Don't feel too badly about this, Jamie," she said. She was saying an awful lot, but all I could properly focus on was the way that she said my name, how it sounded, and how her hands were so much warmer than mine. If I could just be in her presence for the rest of my life, I thought, I would never feel an ounce of upset ever again. I wanted us to be best friends.

"I live in the blue house three streets up," I heard myself saying and felt my lips blurting. I hadn't entirely meant to say it, but now it couldn't be taken back.

Her eyebrows came together again and she laughed, a sound that came from her lungs and rang through her whole chest, spilled from her throat, and filled the barn.

"Is this your way of asking me to come and visit?" she asked, smiling like the Cheshire cat, canines like a wolf's.

"If you would like to. That would be nice."

"That *would* be nice, wouldn't it?"

I nodded, suddenly very eager. I pictured Eleanor in my house, in my garden, wherever she wanted to be.

"I have to finish cleaning right now, but maybe tomorrow."

"Oh! Of course," I shook my head, releasing her hands. "Maybe tomorrow, then."

She stood and picked up her sponge again, going back to scrubbing the blood off of the sword. I watched her in silence for a few minutes before Atticus walked in, pointing a finger in my direction.

"Jamie," he grinned, holding up his arms like he had just won the lottery, "we've got another execution tomorrow."

# FIVE

My second execution was a man named Francis Clarke. He was a tall, lanky man with inky black curls and icy blue eyes, dressed in a blue dress shirt. He stood in front of the block nervously, fiddling with the rope tying his hands together and tapping his foot every now and again. Despite the crowd, the area around the barn was quiet, and his foot tapping echoed terribly in the near-silence.

"Drugs," Atticus told me. His explanation was short and unhelpful, the way one's explanation often had to be when he only had seconds to go before announcing an execution.

Smuggling drugs? Possession of drugs? It didn't answer many questions, but I accepted it.

When he stood up next to Francis he said the same things that he had said before Mary's execution, the same things he had said to Mary. This time, instead of having him shove me onto the concrete block, I made my way up the steps, lowering my hood a little further down, hiding my eyes as if it would do anything to cover up the impending scene, the scene that I was about to be a part of.

Francis got to his knees, less willingly than Mary had, biting his bottom lip, which was scabbed over in some places and freshly bitten and bleeding in others.

"Let me say goodbye to William," he cried as if I knew who William was. I kept quiet, but my stomach dropped, like a rock falling to the bottom of a pond. "Please, just let me… just let me look."

I took a cautious step back, acting as if I were shining my blade while he settled a little in his spot, and found William in the flurry of faces staring up at him.

"Goodbye, my son!" he called out, holding his tied hands up to press his fingers to his lips and waving them out to the crowd. Though there had been a massive turnout for the first execution, that was nothing compared to the second. There were, without question, at least thirty more people tonight than there had been at Mary's execution. A teenage boy, one who looked a bit like Francis, was crying. His arms were wrapped around the shoulders of a woman who may or may not have been his mother. The boy had Francis' black curls and long limbs, a pair of round glasses perched on the bridge of his nose. His mother was a blonde, swan-like woman with eyes so blue that I could pick out the color from my spot at the concrete block.

The boy, who I assumed was William, hid his face in the woman's shoulder and Francis shook his head, tears falling down his face and dripping onto the collar of his shirt, leaving their tracks on his cheeks as a snail does. Silently, shakily, he sat back and laid his head against the block with a grimace.

"Forgive me," I whispered to Francis in the same way that I had whispered to Mary. This time, though, it was more rushed, more frantic. I was fairly sure that he could sense my discomfort, but I knew that he had to have been much more uncomfortable than I was at that moment.

He didn't say anything, head stuck in the same position while I stood over him, trembling just enough to make me wonder if Atticus could see me doing so. Arms shaking, more out of fear than exertion, I raised the sword and steadied it, evened out my breathing, and brought it down. Then came the thunk of the sword against bone and wood, the animalistic cry from Francis before the blade pierced his skin. Another shriek rang out, possibly from Francis' wife, and so did a loud, pained cry.

I had done that, I reminded myself. I was the reason that a wife had lost her husband, that a son had lost his father. When they tried to sleep tonight, they would see Francis' face, contorted in fear, and I would lie awake, knowing that I had done one of the worst things a person could do. I had killed a person. I had killed *two*. I couldn't bring myself to look down at the scene I had created and instead made my way hurriedly back to the barn, dropping my sword in the process.

Slamming the barn door, I shut my eyes tight, folding my hands into fists and resting them upon my forehead as I took a deep breath through my nose. I wished that Eleanor was there to hold my hands as she had the day before. But then, it occurred to me that Eleanor might not want to associate herself with a woman who had just killed somebody, at least not moments after it had happened. Eleanor might not want to be friends with a woman who had begged for this job, been so sure of herself when she had done so, and was now ready to throw it away after the first week. I groaned and thought that perhaps it was selfish of me to think in this manner at all.

I wasn't sure how long I stayed resting against

the wall, folded at the waist and staring at the toes of my shoes, gulping for air like a fish on a deck, but when the door finally did bang open, Atticus was the one who was standing in the doorway, passing me two handfuls of money.

"Jamie, you can't just run away as soon as you've finished. You've got to stay for a moment so you don't look like a coward. It's not good for my business."

I watched him double-check the money and said, very unsteadily, "Mr. Jones, I'm not sure that I can do this any longer."

"Of course you can," he said with a laugh, as if I had made a joke. I shook my head, shoving the money into my pockets.

"This is horrible, and it makes me feel awful. I really am sorry."

It was his turn to shake his head. Somebody, his wife, I assumed, opened the door a crack and handed him the sword. I looked away when I caught a glimpse of the blood dripping from the blade, forming a deep red puddle on the floor. I knew that it would stain, and I knew that I would never feel comfortable in that barn again, that I would never see the floor clean again, whether the stain was actually there or not.

"You wanted this. You came to me, begging.

Give it one more try, Jamie. Just one. There is a woman who needs to be dealt with sooner rather than later, hopefully on Thursday."

I let my head fall back against the wall with a *thump* and released my hands from their fists before shaking them uselessly and balling them back up again.

"How are you so alright with all of this? What Francis did was not something that should have gotten him killed, it should have gotten him medical attention. Do you even know what is punishable by death?" I closed my eyes. "It seems like you just want to take whoever is locked up at the moment and shove them onto the chopping block."

He narrowed his eyes.

"If I remember correctly, Jamie, you were as alright with this as I am, just days ago. Don't you go thinking that now that you're the big, bad executioner, you can speak to me like this. Remember, I control your pay."

"I don't care. I want nothing to do with this anymore."

Atticus picked up a coin that had fallen onto the floor and set it on a haystack, crossing his arms over his chest, face red with fury.

"Go home and think it over," he said roughly, flinging the door open and gesturing for me to leave. "If you still feel like being unemployed by tomorrow morning, then let me know."

I threw my robes off and balled them up, tossing them into the corner of the room where the sword, still unsheathed, was balanced against the wall, before picking up the spare coin and straightening up.

"I certainly will," I growled as I stalked past him and out through the door.

The smell of blood was prominent outdoors, and most of the people who had been watching had already gone home. William, however, was still standing, now closer to the block, with his mother. I tried not to look at Francis' body but wound up doing so anyway.

His head was nowhere in sight, probably removed from the scene by Atticus or his wife, but there was a pool of blood that seemed to flow toward me and follow me back home like a trail of breadcrumbs.

William and his mother had not seemed to notice me. This was probably for the better.

\*\*\*

It took two hours for me to get back home since I kept stopping to take a seat on the side of the road, picturing Francis and William, and William and his mother, and how Francis' features might not have ever slacked but stayed sobbing forever.

When I did get home, however, there was a large brown envelope sitting on my doorstep, blocking the worn letters on the old welcome mat that my grandmother had bought years ago. I brought it inside with me, falling onto the sofa and using my key to rip the envelope open. There was a check inside for a large sum of money, though I had already received what I had been owed, and a handwritten note from Atticus.

*Jamie,*

*I had my wife drop this off, assuming you are home. You might have noticed that I have included a rather large check. After you left, Francis' son drowned himself in the river behind the barn and died. Considering this, I would like to pay you just under double. My apologies for the dark matter of this letter. I wish that I had some better news to deliver.*

*Atticus Jones*

Died?
Died.

I read it three times more before letting the check and the letter fall onto the floor. William had still been so young, seventeen at most. I thought, watching the ceiling grow black as the moon rose higher in the sky, of how he would never marry, never have children, never live a full life.

Weakly, I pulled myself up and made my way to the kitchen, where I began to boil water in my largest pot. I paced back and forth as it boiled, eyes fixed on my feet and thumbnail lodged between my teeth, and dumped pots into the bathtub every few minutes. My hands were sticky, probably from sweat, but it felt much stickier than that. When I glanced down, I noticed that the residual blood from the sword had left its marks on my palms.

Breathing fast, I watched my reflection in the mirror as I pulled off my clothes. My cheeks were turning pink and my bangs curled from the humidity. Standing at the sink in nothing but my underwear, I felt a deep sense of something following me, watching me through the tiny bathroom window. The feeling unfurled in my stomach as I crawled into the tub and curled into myself, desperately trying to scrub the blood from my palms. The harder I scrubbed, the more blood appeared, and eventually, I was left sitting in water that was tinted pink, letting it pool in my cupped hands.

I sobbed, rising to my knees and bracing one hand against the wall, the water around me growing darker. The feeling in my stomach that had unfurled now shifted, a pang of gnawing guilt and desperation to reverse the whole situation making its way into my chest, into the cavity between my lungs.

That night, for the first time in seven years, I knelt with my head bowed, dripping from the bath, hands bloody, and prayed.

# SIX

It was early when I woke, too early to call it morning, too late to call it night. My bedroom was covered in a thick layer of black. There was not an ounce of light except for the sliver of light from the crescent moon peering through the curtains.

I rolled over in bed, closing my eyes again and adjusting the pillow beneath my head. I shivered as goosebumps made their way over my skin. The sheets were cold, and so were my arms, and I pulled the covers further up around my shoulders, sighing deeply.

A faint rustling noise sounded from somewhere in my bedroom, and I realized that this noise was what had woken me in the first place. I pulled myself up into a sitting position and looked around, eyes finally adjusting to the dark. There was nothing wrong in the room, nothing out of place, nobody else in it with me. The rustling sounded again, and once more, and I stood with a shiver, making my way to the window to throw the curtains back. I squinted at the harsh light of the moon, nose wrinkling involuntarily. When I blinked away the dots of light that clouded my vision, my breath caught in my throat, and something in my body shifted. Somewhere deep in my bones, or in my heart, or in my brain, I was certain that I would never feel settled again, and that nothing would ever be the same.

Standing in the middle of the cornfield was Francis, his head tilted toward his left shoulder, blood dripping down his neck, hooking his collarbone, and disappearing into the collar of his shirt. His eyes were milky white, nose and mouth bloody, skin broken and pale like an eggshell. Beside him was William, glasses shattered, eyes just as white as his father's. His lips were faded, soft purple around the edges, cracked and bloody, skin tinted icy blue. Spidery veins were broken around his eyes, and his head was hanging a little, angled to the right. He was dripping, a puddle of water pooling at his feet and soaking through his shoes. He looked at Francis, who nodded, a little solemnly, and they looked back at me in unison and raised their hands as if it was their first time meeting me.

My heart stuttered, but as hard as I tried, I couldn't seem to pull my eyes away from them. Something about the scene before me was both haunting and fascinating. It was like looking at a trainwreck, when you know that you should look the other way, but you have never seen something so disturbing and upsetting, and you just have to know what will happen next. It occurred to me, then, that this must have been how the people felt while watching the executions. The sick wonder and awe, the desire to understand how it works, the grief for others and the relief that it isn't happening to you, and the numbness that follows. It must have been addicting.

I wondered when the relief and numbness would kick in, because, standing frozen in front of the window, looking out at the cornfield behind my house, I was ready to quit my job, all the money be damned.

A cold wash of fear crept its way through my veins and into my bones, straight through the marrow, running down my spine and causing me to shiver.

I thought I should apologize to them, so I mouthed an apology. But Francis only narrowed his eyes, and William simply tilted his head further to the side in question. Their arms were still stretched toward me, hands splayed wide open, fingers long and thin like the branches of the trees clawing at my window. They seemed to say, *just come with us. You know that it would be easier.*

I considered this for a long moment. It would, I thought, be so much easier. But, I would never see Eleanor again if I were dead, and if Heaven were real, surely there was no way that I would ever be allowed in.

"I'm sorry, I'm sorry, I'm sorry," I said. I repeated it over and over until the words sounded unfamiliar, became useless, and jumbled, and my tongue grew heavy in my mouth.

The two men continued to stare, through my body and my soul. I forced myself to turn away, and steadied myself against my desk, taking a seat in my chair. There was a cushion from my grandmother's sofa sitting against its back. I thrust it onto my bed. My grandmother would not have wanted her cushion to aid my nervous breakdown, much less one that was my own fault. I pulled the stub of a pencil from my pencil pot and tore a piece of paper from my notebook, pulling my hair back into a bun at the base of my neck and scribbling furiously:

*Mr. Jones,*

*I have come to the difficult decision to resign from my position as City Executioner. I appreciate the opportunity that you have given me, but I cannot persist in this career path. My sincerest apologies. Thank you.*

*Jamie Foster*

Setting down my pencil, I folded the paper in half and rooted through my desk to find an envelope. The one that I did manage to find was stained with tea in the top right corner, but I figured that Atticus probably would not care all that much. I sealed it and turned it over, writing Atticus' name on the back in large, looping letters, and stared at it for a moment. I stared hard enough that I silently, foolishly, hoped to burn a hole straight through the letter, through the entire situation.

"That's it," I whispered. When I glanced up, Francis and William had disappeared. I let out a breath of relief and pulled my jacket and shoes on. If I delivered the letter this late at night, I would not have had to face an outraged Atticus when he found out in the morning. Without a second thought, I threw the door open and marched out into the night.

The air was cold, far colder than it should have been for this early in November. There was an icy sort of atmosphere outdoors like I had walked into a meat locker. Though I was beginning to sweat—I wasn't entirely sure whether it was from the adrenaline rush or the fear—the sweat seemed to freeze and form snowflakes, sitting upon my skin and melting into my blood. This might have been alright, if it were not for the sight before me, the sight that made my blood truly run cold.

"I said that I was sorry," I said quietly, looking helplessly at Francis and William, who were now standing mere feet from me, watching me like lions watching their prey. Francis smiled, a little sadly, and shrugged. William opened his mouth, and a trickle of water fell down his front and added to the puddle beneath him.

"You killed my father," he said simply. His words were gurgled, and he sounded as if he had swallowed a handful of rocks.

"I didn't want to."

"And yet, you did it anyway."

There was something about the way he spoke that caused my eyes to burn with tears and broke a small part of me, something buried deep inside my chest. He spoke with an air of naivety, a simplicity that was often reserved for children, and an innocence that had been ripped from me long ago.

"I did, but I didn't want to. You have to understand that."

Francis' voice, soft and low, came next.

"It didn't hurt as badly as I had imagined, you know," he told me, like a teacher trying to calm a crying child. "It was quick. Just like that."

He snapped his delicate fingers with one hand and made a cut-throat motion with the other.

This was the final straw, it seemed, because my tears finally sprang forward, and I took a breath to will them to stay behind my eyes. "I have decided to quit. I will never do it again. I promise."

"That can't help us any," Francis murmured, tilting his head up to look at the moon. Of course, I knew this. But, it would help the others who were supposed to be after him.

"It was very cold," William said thoughtfully as he straightened up a little. "That lake was *very* cold. You should speak to somebody about it."

"Now, what would your mama think of that, son? She can't be too happy with you, is she?" Francis remarked.

My breath hitched, and I bit down hard on my bottom lip to stifle a cry, so hard that blood bloomed beneath my teeth. I turned back around, slamming the door and locking away Francis and William.

There was no way that I could give Atticus my letter now. I thrust the envelope onto the table and sat down, the kitchen window's curtains drawn closed, with my head in my hands. I thought about William's words all night long.

I had not wanted to do any of it, that was true. But even truer was that I had done it anyway.

\*\*\*

When I returned to a restless sleep, I dreamt of something shining and golden, and of wide eyes, and constellations made up of freckles. I was unsure of what I was looking at, until I reached out to a hand as pale as bone, one with magnificently pink knuckles and fingertips, and brushed the wrist to whom the hand belonged. The fingers of the hand gravitated toward mine, lowered just a touch until our fingers were mirrored. Our fingerprints would stamp into each other and fade by the time the sun rose, but, I thought, just this one touch would be more than enough. There came a sizzling between our hands, our wrists, and suddenly, wrapped around our pinky fingers, a single, fragile, thread of gold, a magnetic pull that could not be ignored. My pointer finger slowly crept forward, inch by inch, just enough to feel the heat of another body in front of mine.

I woke slumped over the table, one hand reaching out into the empty kitchen.

## SEVEN

The next morning, my face was sticky and stiff, and my head pounded dully near the base of my skull.

I rose from the chair where I had fallen asleep the night before and drank a glass of water while I waited for the kettle to boil. Sipping idly, I stood in the window and reached for the curtains with my heart in my throat, rubbing the rough fabric between my thumb and pointer finger as I hesitated. But, when I shoved them open, nothing was out of the ordinary. Nobody was standing in the cornfield or outside the front door, not even the crows who normally spent their mornings watching me eat my breakfast.

I wondered for a moment if I had dreamt it all, or if it had been real. Had they been ghosts? Or were they a product of my brain spiraling downwards?

After drinking my tea and forcing a slice of dry toast down my throat, I retrieved my letter to Atticus, the only physical proof I had of the events of the night before, and walked to the farmhouse.

I rubbed my hands against one another as I walked. It was cold enough that my breath formed tiny puffs of smoke in the dull gray morning sky. Remnants of rain from the night before still hung in the air, light precipitation that made the ground smell like wet soil. I walked tensely, feeling as if I had a wooden plank for a spine, part of my mind waiting for Francis or William to show up as I passed the train tracks or wandered through the wooded path. I felt the same as I had when I was a little girl, playing hide-and-seek with my little cousins, rounding corners cautiously, having to steel myself as I did so. A crow let out a throaty caw from someplace in the distance and I jumped, heart pounding and blood rushing in my ears.

At least, I thought, it would all be over after today. Once I gave my letter to Atticus, I would never have to do this again, and the guilt would leave along with my employment. However, when I arrived at the barn, Atticus was, once again, nowhere to be seen. I stepped into the barn, greeted by Eleanor, who was feeding a sugar cube to one of the horses, smiling fondly as it licked the palm of her hand. My sword was leaning against the wall, unsheathed and thickly caked in a layer of browning blood. At the sight, I turned away and swallowed with difficulty.

"Hello," she said, looking up from the horse to meet my eyes. "Well, you look terrible."

I flushed, letting out a surprised laugh. "Thank you, Eleanor."

"No, really."

Her light brows were knit, lips turned downward in a frown. She patted the horse on the head twice and wiped her palms in her black skirt before making her way over to me, resting one hand on my cheek and the other near my chin. I was fairly sure that my cheeks were still red, and at the sudden touch, grew redder, though I was unsure why. My chest was growing fluttery, and I tried not to cringe.

"I'm alright, I swear," I assured her. She bit her lip but dropped her hands and sat down on a haystack toward the back of the barn. I nearly sighed in relief when she backed away, at once aware of how long it had been since I had felt somebody else's touch.

"What is that?" she asked as I came to sit with

her, gesturing in the direction of the envelope in my hand.

"My letter of resignation."

"Your letter of resignation?"

I nodded. "Where is Atticus? I need to give this to him as soon as I possibly can."

Eleanor went back to frowning. I wished that she would do something else. "He's at his father-in-law's house with his daughters." she eyed me carefully, folding her arms over her chest. "Florence is home if you'd like to speak with her."

"Maybe. I think I would rather speak to him directly."

"Why are you in such a rush to get it to him?" she asked.

I wanted to call her out for being nosy, but I was a nosy person myself, so I held myself back. Instead, I said, "I can't tell you. You'll think I'm mad."

Eleanor scoffed, scooting a little closer to me and swinging her legs. "I will not think that you're mad. I promise it."

"You can't promise that, Eleanor. This is strange. I don't even know if it was real."

Eleanor took both of my hands, just as she had done before. I looked down but allowed her to keep my hands in hers. Our knees were touching now that we were so close together. She sat directly in front of me, taking up all of the space in my vision. She took one hand away and placed it on my cheek, as light as a feather, directing my face upward to meet her eyes. They were so wide and dark and deep that I was sure I could drown in them.

"Jamie. I want to help you, and I can't do that if you don't tell me what's wrong." Her voice was soft, and I wondered if it was from all of her years spent dealing with children, or if she just spoke this way with everybody. "I will believe you. You do know that, don't you?"

"How are you so good at this?" I asked suddenly. She laughed a little.

"Good at what?"

"This. Caring. I don't feel scared around you."

She squeezed my hand a little tighter. "You should never have to feel scared in the first place. Besides, I'm only caring because I *do* care about you."

I shook my head. "Why?"

"*Why?*"

"Yes. We've only just met, and it's not as though I've done something to make you care about me, have I? I'm not anything extraordinary."

Eleanor's light brows came together and her head tilted to the side in a movement that seemed involuntary. She let out a breath and bit at the inside of her cheek, looking as though she was choosing her next words carefully.

"You don't have to do things for people to *make* them care about you, Jamie. And you don't have to be extraordinary. That isn't how it works. I care about you because you're my friend, and you can come to me whenever you need me," she said, rather sadly.

"Are you sure?"

"Yes, I'm sure."

I looked at the ceiling, at the damp spots that looked like scars from where there had been leaks in the past, then back at Eleanor. I hung my head so that I would not have to look at her as I spoke.

"Last night I woke up and thought that I saw Francis and William Clark. The ones who died yesterday. I did see them, I'm sure of it. They were standing outside my bedroom window, and they were watching me, and I was so afraid that I decided to quit. I wanted to deliver my letter as soon as it was written, but they were outside my front door, and they started speaking to me. I tried to tell them that I hadn't wanted to do it, but William said, *and yet, you did it anyway.*" I took a deep breath. "Then I realized that, yes, I did. It doesn't matter at all how much it hurts me. Just imagine how much it hurts everybody else."

Eleanor was staring at me by the time I had finished, still holding onto one of my shaking hands.

"You're positively sure that it wasn't a dream?" she asked cautiously.

"Yes. I know that it was real."

"You don't believe in ghosts, do you?"

"Not entirely," I said.

She smiled a little. "Me neither."

I shrugged. "So, what could it have been, then?"

"Hallucinations? Something like that, maybe. Just take a breath, first." Her voice was impossibly soft.

I took a breath through my nose and let it out through my lips. "You don't think that I'm mad?"

"I think," she said slowly, "that you are under far too much pressure at the moment, and that if quitting is what you need to do to feel better, then you should do it."

She hadn't exactly said that she did not think I was going mad, but she hadn't said that she thought I *was*, either.

Having somebody on my side, though, felt alright.

***

Eleanor and I sat out in the damp grass later that day. It must have been nearing two o'clock in the afternoon, but I had no intention of going back home any time soon, and neither, it seemed, did Eleanor.

She was lying on her back with her arms pillowed behind her head and one leg kicked out. Her hair was spread out around her, like rays of sun surrounding her head, and her nose and cheeks were pink from the cold. I sat cross-legged beside her, fiddling absentmindedly with the lace on one of her shoes.

"My brother fell right through the ice, into the lake," she was saying with a smile, telling me a story about how she and her brother had tried to go ice skating without skates as children. "I had to pull him out, and the water was freezing."

"Were your parents there?" I asked. "Were they angry with you?"

Her face shuttered and the smile fell from her lips, but she said, "No, we went out alone often. They were busy."

Sensing that this was a sensitive subject, I asked instead, "Have you ever ridden a horse?"

"No," she laughed, her smile back as quickly as

it had gone. "I would love to someday, though."

"I rode one when I was little. I must have been seven because it was before my parents started traveling. Anyway, I was sitting on it, this little brown horse, and it took off running so quickly that I nearly fell off. I was afraid of horses for years after."

"That's a shame," Eleanor said, lips pursed. "I really would like to ride one."

"We could try convincing Atticus to let us ride one of his," I suggested, though I knew that it would never work.

Eleanor snorted and laughed, "Keep dreaming, Love."

The more time I spent with Eleanor, the more I noticed the remnants of an accent in her voice, one that sounded a bit English, but not quite. She must have lived somewhere near England for some time. It seemed as if she had lost the majority of her accent long ago.

Curious, I asked, "Are you from England?"

"Wales. I only lived there when I was a baby and a toddler, but most of my family was Welsh. I picked up the accent as a child, but it never really went away."

"I think it's quite pretty."

She shot me a funny grin. We sat in silence for a

few minutes before she sprung up onto her knees quickly, gathering her skirt onto her lap and pointing excitedly at something in the distance.

"There's a cat!" she exclaimed with a wide smile, patting the ground next to her. The cat, large and white, with a belly so big that it nearly brushed the ground beneath it, bravely made its way over to her and allowed her to scoop it up in her arms. She looked at it in adoration, scratching under its chin and behind its ears.

"It must be a stray," I said as I held out my pointer finger in its direction. It sniffed my hand and chewed happily on my finger, and I let it.

"I love cats," Eleanor mused, taking its fat, fluffy face in her hands and laughing. "My aunt Clara had one when I was a child."

"What was it like?" I asked, rubbing the cat on the forehead.

And so she told me about her aunt Clara's cat while we played with the stray, just us three out in the field until the sun began to set. By then, I had forgotten all about the night before, had even forgotten where I was and why I had come here. The world grew narrower and narrower, until it consisted of Eleanor, and Eleanor alone.

# EIGHT

On my second day off, I spent the afternoon working in the garden near the cornfield. There had been lettuce and cabbage seeds sitting on my kitchen counter for months that I had yet to plant, and other plants desperately needed watering. After my day with Eleanor, I felt a bit more at ease— at least, comfortable enough to spend time alone outside.

I was kneeling in the dirt, wearing a pair of brown trousers with wide legs and a gray-blue blouse tucked into the waistband. My shoes would need to be rinsed later, and I would have to wash my pants as soon as I went indoors, if the feeling of wet soil soaking through my knees was any indication, but it all felt worth it to watch my plants grow.

It was a quiet afternoon, the low chirping and trilling of the birds being the only real sound around me. I was bringing a worm to a family of blackbirds nearby when a figure stepped out from around the front of the house. It was, to my surprise, Eleanor, with her hair half-tied back with a black ribbon, wearing a dark brown skirt and a white button-up.

"Hi," I greeted as I dropped the worm at my feet, stunned.

"Hello," she said, eyeing the worm with an awkward smile. "I'm sorry to barge in like this. I should have asked."

I wiped my hands on the legs of my pants and shook my head. "No, that's alright. I'm just planting some vegetables. Would you like some tea?"

She followed me back to the garden and waited next to my pile of soil while I dragged a chair out from the kitchen for her to sit on. She flung one leg over the other and smoothed out her skirt a bit.

"I'm fine, thank you."

I knelt back down and picked up my spade. "What brings you here, then?"

"I just wanted to see you, I suppose." Eleanor shrugged.

"Well, that certainly isn't a crime."

"Surely not," she grinned, twisting a strand of

hair around her pointer finger. I looked up to meet her eyes. She was watching me with something akin to wonder, one elbow resting on her knee with her chin in the palm of her hand.

"Do you garden?" I asked.

This sparked a sharp laugh, and she readjusted herself in the chair so that she was sitting more comfortably, like she planned on being here for a while. "Not at all. I have tried, but I manage to kill everything. I do wish that I could keep just one nice bunch of flowers, honestly."

I held up a handful of seeds to show her and made a rather big deal of putting them into the holes I had been digging, then covered them up gently. My hands were growing stiff from the watery mud drying into them.

"That's it. It isn't too difficult, once you learn to do it."

Eleanor's eyes were full of amusement as she asked, "How did you learn to do it? My aunt wanted to plant roses with me, once, but she died before she could."

"My mother had a massive green thumb. She taught me to garden when I was little. My father was not nearly as talented, but he tried," I smiled sadly. "We gardened a lot. Then they died, so my grandmother started this garden as a way to remember my mother. I've been tending to it since she died."

"It's nice that you're still doing it," she said, swinging her legs a little. This was something that I had noticed she tended to do while sitting. She seemed completely unable to sit still. "I'm sorry about them, though. Your grandmother and your parents. It's hard to grow up without them."

My chest tightened. "I did grow up with them, mostly. They died when I was eight, so at least I got to spend some time with them. My grandmother took wonderful care of me, as well."

Eleanor's expression turned into something complicated for a millisecond, but she replaced her smile so quickly that I wondered if I had simply imagined it. "That's good."

"Did your—um…" I cleared my throat and shook my head. "You mentioned that you took care of your brother a lot as a child?"

Eleanor's cheeks flushed, but she smiled softly and tugged her sleeves over her hands.

"I think I might take you up on your offer for tea and tell you about it then. It could take a while."

\*\*\*

I put the kettle on and went through the pantry to find a package of stale biscuits, and left Eleanor alone in the kitchen while I went to my bedroom to change my pants. When I returned, she was sitting at the table with one leg thrown over the other while she ate a biscuit.

"Jamie," she said as I pulled two teacups from the cupboard. "My childhood is messy. I want you to know that you can tell me to stop talking whenever you would like me to. I know that not everybody wants to hear about this kind of thing."

I poured up the tea, glancing at her over my shoulder. "Don't worry. You don't have to tell me about it if you aren't comfortable, but I won't think of you any differently. I promise."

"Alright…" She took a sip of tea and waited for me to sit down. "Well, my mother died when I was two years old. I don't remember it at all. When she died, my father became secluded and upset." She inhaled deeply and looked down. "I suppose he was just angry, and he had no other way to get his anger out. That's what I always told myself, anyway."

My stomach clenched, and I set down my teacup. "Eleanor."

"He didn't hit me often. He—" she blew out a breath and looked at the ceiling. "He told me that everybody hit their kids, and I knew that a lot of them did, so I didn't think that it was a problem. I just didn't know that most kids don't get thrown around to that extent until I started going to school."

Eleanor paused, waiting for me to interrupt or ask a question, but I had nothing to say. She played with the crumbs on her plate and continued.

"He remarried when I was four years old, when we moved from Wales to Saint Louis. My brother, Joseph, was born later that year. My father and his wife wanted little to do with him after my father messed up Joseph's hip. That's when I began taking care of him."

My brain was working quickly, trying to process everything that she was telling me.

"It started to get really bad when I was thirteen, maybe. That was when I knew that I needed to get us away. I didn't want Joseph to be hurt any more than he already had been, but I was also tired of being hurt. I got a job, saved my money, and he and I moved here on my eighteenth birthday. We lived together until last year. Then, he moved a few hours away, but I still see him often enough."

She was carefully avoiding my eyes, and I leaned back in my chair, watching the steam roll off the tea in my cup.

"That's a lot for one little girl," I said finally. Eleanor shrugged, but her eyes had grown glossy, lips pressed tightly together, though she was clearly trying to smile.

"What can you do, right?" she sighed, laughing uneasily.

"I'm sorry for having you relive all of that. I didn't mean to..." I gestured vaguely with my hands. Eleanor took another bite of her biscuit.

"It's not your fault, Jamie. You couldn't have known."

"I'm still sorry."

The house was quiet for a moment, until Eleanor spoke again, voice suddenly wobbly and deprived of any of her usual softness.

"It just makes me angry. It makes me angry that Joseph had to grow up without any love from his parents. He got *nothing*. That isn't fair."

I reached slowly across the table, frowning as I placed my hands over Eleanor's.

"It wasn't fair to either of you, Eleanor. Not just him. You suffered, too."

Eleanor squeezed my hand lightly and sniffled. "I suppose."

I rose from my chair and made my way to where she was sitting across from me, standing behind her chair to wrap my arms around her neck. She reached up and wrapped her arms around mine, resting her cheek in the crook of my arm.

"I felt so alone, Jamie," she said, voice muffled and wet.

I wanted to say something, anything, but there was nothing that I could say to fix any of this. I wanted to tell her that none of it was her fault, not in the least, that what she endured meant no less than what her brother had, and that everything was going to be alright.

I couldn't promise that last bit, though, so I settled for sighing.

"You don't have to worry about being alone anymore," I said. Her breath hitched as she stifled tears, but she nodded. "I promise."

That was one promise that I could make.

"Thank you," she whispered, tightening her grip on my arms.

"You don't need to thank me."

"I want to, though."

I smiled, just a bit, and held her a little tighter. Normally, if I was being honest, seeing somebody cry made me want to run away. I did not even want to be with myself when I cried. I had always been rather useless when it came to comfort, to anything regarding my feelings or those of others. But Eleanor did not make me want to run.

"Thank you, too," I whispered. "I've never really had a friend before. I don't quite know what to do."

She nodded again, and I felt her breathe shakily against me.

"This is more than enough."

# NINE

There was a dream that I used to have as a child after my parents died, one where I was watching them drowning from the shore, screaming for help, but I didn't know how to swim. When nobody came to save them, I got into the water myself and tried to swim to where they were sinking. I can still remember their eyes in that dream, the horror in their faces, because I was drowning, myself, in the act of trying to save them.

"Jamie, no!" they would scream, sometimes in unison, sometimes one or the other. "*You're* going to drown!"

"You're going to drown!" I would yell right back. I knew from the way that my father's grip on my mother loosened that it was going to happen soon.

"We already have," my mother would call gently, giving me a shove. This shove was enough to send me flying back to the shore, where I would sit, crying, unable to do anything but watch as the waves swallowed them whole.

Each time I woke from this dream, my heart pounded with an intensity that had me convinced that I might die, too, but I was not necessarily upset about this thought.

I'm still not sure why the dream was so frequent, what it meant, why the dream could never end happily, or why I thought that I could save them in the first place.

I do know, though, that the night before my third execution, I dreamt this dream again.

***

Anne Shelley was being executed for treason. Foolishly, I didn't know, before this execution, what treason meant.

Standing behind the barn with Atticus, I watched, horrified, as Anne stood calmly before the block, nose in the air as she watched the crowd in front of her.

"Treason? Do you have proof?" I asked. He looked at me with his eyebrows raised, as if I were asking him to give me a grand tour of the barn animals.

"The government does. That's quite enough for me, and it should be enough for you."

*The government is in shambles, Jones*, I wanted to say. Instead, I clenched my jaw as hard as I could, so hard that my ears began to ache.

"My resignation is on my kitchen table, Mr. Jones," I said instead. "I'm telling you, I don't think that I'm cut out for this any longer."

Atticus' arms came to his chest and he folded them, feet planted on the muddy ground where the grass had yellowed and was beginning to frost over.

"You weren't cut out for it in the first place. I knew it all along. I've known it since I gave you the damn job, Foster. You haven't got the guts."

"It's not that I don't think that people should be punished for their crimes. I just don't think that I can be the one to do it. Find somebody else."

Atticus laughed coldly. "After today, I certainly will."

He left and ran through his usual routine, introducing Anne and stating her crime, ushering me onto the concrete block and stepping back into the safety of the barn to watch.

"Please forgive me," I whispered, fighting the urge to lower myself to her level. Peter, who

I hadn't seen since the first execution, was standing in the crowd, frowning severely. It crossed my mind, as I lifted the sword, that more and more people were attending every execution. I looked, but I still didn't see Eleanor. Not that I blamed her. If I were not the one performing the execution, I might not come either.

Anne's eyes were determined, chin set, and lips pressed together as she knelt before the block. She did not speak, unlike Mary and Francis. It seemed that she had accepted it and did not wish to think about it any longer.

I took one last look at the people who were watching, chanting an apology over and over in my head and hanging onto the words like a lifeline. I considered praying again right then and there.

*I'm sorry, I'm sorry, I'm sorry, I'm sorry.*

I brought down the sword, trying as hard as I possibly could to ignore the *thunk* of the metal against wood, the screams toward the front of the crowd, and the squelch of blood and flesh. Anne's head thumped against the ground.

*I'm sorry, I'm sorry, I'm sorry, I'm sorry.*

I didn't spare a glance at Anne's body, instead fleeing back to the barn, knocking my shoulder against Atticus' on the way and dropping my sword with a clatter. I shed my robes and balled them up on the floor. Faintly, I heard Atticus speaking. He must have been standing in front of the crowd like he was an announcer awaiting a performer.

"Ladies and gentlemen! We are now responsible for the most executions in Kansas, in history!"

That was enough for me to decide that I was ready to begin the walk back home. I shuffled around the haystacks and went through the side door, which was not used often and creaked when it opened, to avoid the crowds. It worked, somewhat, as only a few onlookers spared glances and whispers as I broke free and started on the walk home.

*** 

On my way, a tall, slender man with a graying beard and a blonde lady on his arm stopped me.

"Miss!" he called. I ignored him, picking up my pace and deliberately looking straight ahead. He called out again and I turned around to face him. "Are you the executioner?"

I nodded and looked around.

"That was my sister who you just killed. As far as I know, she didn't do a thing."

I shook my head. "I'm sorry, sir. I'm very sorry. I was not aware—"

"No," he interrupted, walking toward me so

that I was standing up against a tree, bark digging into my back. "No, you little—"

"Allan, that is quite enough!" the blonde lady called.

He whipped around quickly and hissed a low, "Shut your mouth!" in her direction. She shrunk back and met my eyes apologetically.

"Are you afraid?" he asked quietly.

I stared at him, confused. Of course, I was afraid. Did he want me to be afraid?

"I asked you if you're afraid," he growled.

I nodded quickly, breathing picking up. It was the right answer and it was the raw truth.

"I think that you should have thought that over before you killed my Anne," he said slowly, voice gravelly and threatening as he reached into his coat pocket. My body stiffened, heart plummeting as I shot a helpless look at the lady behind me.

"Allan, don't!" she shouted.

"Judy, stop talking, you *twat!*" he produced a kitchen knife from his pocket and held it up, running his thumb along the blade. I squeezed my eyes shut.

"Don't you dare!" her voice rose an octave, shrill and urgent. Allan remained still, but his eye twitched, growing more annoyed as he gazed at me threateningly. "Allan, I will leave you!"

"Look away if you want to! For God's sake..." his cheeks were turning red, hands beginning to tremble. My own were doing the same, and I moved them so that they were balled up at my sides.

"I will tell the sheriff," Judy said. Her voice was stern and set, and Allan seemed to gather that she really would tell the sheriff. Still, he turned away from me with his teeth bared and glared in her direction.

"You would never," he snarled, his pug-like face twisted in anger.

"I will walk right down to that station myself and tell him if you do not put that knife down right now."

This made him freeze. I wondered, for a moment, why he was so afraid of the sheriff, but I didn't have time to ponder on this. He threw his knife to the ground, and it landed beside my feet, hitting the base of the tree as he swore under his breath. He took one last glance at me before making his way back to Judy, who flinched away from him.

"Get away from me, you madman. I'll be spending the night at Dorothy's."

I wanted to stay there to make sure that she got away safely, but, perhaps selfishly, I instead grabbed the knife, stuck it in the pocket of my coat, and walked away so quickly that my legs began to burn.

Later that night, I told myself, I would check in at the station and make sure that nothing had happened to her. But until then, I would hide out at home.

Around nine o'clock, I lay in bed and stared at the flame of my candle with dry, gritty eyes. They itched from how hard I fought to keep them from closing. But, I knew that if I let them close, I would just see everything again. I would see Allan and his knife, Anne and her set chin, Francis and William and their blank, glassy eyes.

Sleep can only be fought for so long.

## TEN

As hard as I tried not to fall asleep that night, terrified of the inevitable, I did so in the early hours of the morning, when the sky was still dark and the moon was shining through the curtains like an eerie night light. I slept soundly at first, uninterrupted and comfortable. I should have known that it would not last.

When I woke, there were rustling sounds coming from the cornfield again. At first, somewhat paralyzed by fear, I lay stiff and still, careful not to move an inch as I listened to the noises from outside the window.

I knew better than to investigate, but I also knew that I would be unable to sleep until I saw for myself what was outdoors, like a small part of me was clinging onto the hope that it might be a stray dog or a coyote.

I stood and held my breath while slowly, listening to the floorboards creaking underneath my feet, I walked to the window where I hesitantly drew the curtains back and stared at Francis and William's figures. They were nearly the same as before. The only difference was that this time, Anne had joined them. She was staring straight ahead at me with an unsettling air of calmness, one similar to how she had acted at the execution. Her brown hair was hanging like yarn around her pale face, which was somewhere between green and white. Her eyes were white and foggy, her throat coated in blood that ran down her front, and her body unharmed but covered in bloodstains. She was slumped over, shoulders hunched, like a brunette Raggedy Ann doll.

Anne was still, except for her lips, which were moving clearly and slowly, and though the window was closed, I could still hear her speak.

"I know that you did not want to do it."

In the back of my mind, I was reassured, but this reassurance faded quickly when Francis and William began taking small, slow steps toward the window. I prayed that they would not show up inside of the house, and turned away, drawing the curtains with such speed and force that they made a *snap*.

I wished that I could yell out to somebody who would know what to do. I was both afraid to make a noise and all too aware that nobody would believe me or be able to help me.

"I know that you did not want to do it," Anne said again, and I turned back to the window and peeled the curtains back just a crack. I sobbed, chest growing tight, as I watched Anne press her face against the window, so close that her lips left markings and her breath fogged up the glass when she said, again, "I know that you did not want to do it."

"I'm still sorry," I said. Where had Francis and William gone? I was not going to move to find out.

"I forgive you," she said, voice echoey. "They might, too."

I inhaled deeply, eyes blurry and throat raw. "Thank you."

She remained watching me through the window, white eyes wandering over me, and I felt as if she were taking in the bedroom around me, getting a feel for my bed and a place in my wardrobe, where the three of them would surely find a cozy spot to hide between my dresses and shirts.

I left her where she was and went to the bathroom, the only place where I was sure to find any ounce of solitude. The window in the bathroom was so small that I could barely see the trees outside. My heart was racing, chest heaving as I shut the door with shaking hands and struggled to lock it behind me.

It seemed as if I could still hear her, the wobbly voice fresh in my ears. I had no idea where the other two had gone, and that was not comforting, either.

I climbed into the bathtub, shedding my bed jacket and curled up into a ball. Just as my breathing began to even out, the doorknob jiggled once, then twice. It stilled, then jiggled once more.

There was nothing that I could do except press a fist to my lips to quiet myself and shut my eyes as hard as I could, and I knew it. There was no way to stop anybody from entering if they could open the locked door, which they could, it seemed, because when I opened my eyes, William and Francis were standing over the bathtub. William was dripping water onto the bathmat.

"I'm sorry!" I shouted. "I'm sorry, I told you!"

"Are you sorry?" Francis spoke for the first time that night. "We don't want you to be afraid, really."

"I *am* sorry."

William reached out, and for a moment, looked as if he wanted to touch my face. I flinched away, and instead, he flexed his fingers, watching with something like wonder, and looked at me curiously.

"I can still move just fine," he observed in awe.

"We are not here to frighten you, Jamie."

The way William said my name sent chills shooting down my spine, making their way down my legs and numbing the balls of my feet. Unable to help myself, I turned around.

"Then why are you here?" I asked, looking at the wall.

When I received no response, I slowly turned around to find the bathroom empty and the door closed and locked, just as it had been before. There was no puddle of water on the bathmat.

I took a shaky breath in and wrapped my arms around my knees, turning back around and curling into myself.

The sound of my own breathing and an unexpected train making its way down the tracks were all there was to be heard for the rest of the night. No frogs, no coyotes, nothing but me and that train, and once Anne, William, and Francis had gone, I was left completely alone in my bathtub.

After that, I fell asleep to the echo of my heartbeat in my ears, watching the little window above the sink sweat with condensation, water rolling down its face. I waited for the next sound. For the first time in my life, I noticed how much I feared silence.

## ELEVEN

As soon as I woke the next morning, I got dressed and went to the barn. I knew that Eleanor was meant to be working that day, and if anybody could help me, it was her.

"Eleanor," I huffed breathlessly in the doorway of the barn. "It happened again."

She jumped a little and dropped her sponge as she looked up at me. I winced when I saw the sword but took a step further into the barn.

"What happened again?" she asked, taking my hand and leading me to the haystacks. I took a seat and drew a deep breath.

"I saw William and Francis again. What did you call them?"

"Hallucinations?"

"Yes. I saw them again last night," I explained

as Eleanor retrieved her sponge from where it was lying on the floor. "Anne was there last night, though. The woman I executed yesterday."

Eleanor went quiet for a moment, her cleaning coming to a halt. She quickly started again, though, and looked back at me.

"Anne was there?" she said, scrubbing the sword. She worked with a sort of intensity that I was almost certain stemmed from stress. I could nearly see the cogs in her brain working behind her eyes.

"She was, but it was strange..." I poked my head around the barn door to make sure that Atticus wasn't outside. "She said that she forgave me. She kept saying it, over and over."

Eleanor set the sword and sponge down and took a seat next to me, her bottom lip wedged between her teeth.

"Maybe that's just it," she said, running a hand through her hair.

"What?"

"Maybe it's because she and Mary accepted it. They forgave you, and they had both come to terms with what was going to happen. Francis struggled, right?"

"That was *not* his fault," I argued.

"I didn't say that it was," she said patiently.

"I'm just saying that, perhaps, the fact that you know that they forgave you for what happened is keeping these… hallucinations, or whatever they are, at bay."

She was speaking to me like I was a child, and a very small part of me wanted to scream. However, I knew that she was probably right. She often was, it seemed.

"Maybe that is it," I reasoned. "Can I ask you something?"

Eleanor's cheeks turned a touch red, but it had gone as quickly as it had appeared. It must have been a flush from the cold in the barn.

"Of course you can."

"Why have you not come to any of the executions?"

"I came to the first one."

"Yes, but that was the last. Not that I blame you, of course, but it seems as if more and more people attend each time, and you haven't shown up."

Eleanor sighed through her nose and pursed her lips, tipping her head back to look at the ceiling as she pressed her back against the wall.

"Well, of course, there is the not wanting to see an execution happen. I don't wish to ignore it, but I don't feel as if I need to watch it happen myself. The first one gave me nightmares, and I just couldn't bring myself to go back." She paused, waiting for me to respond, but I didn't, so she continued. "There is more to it, though. Mostly, I don't want to go, because I do not want to think of you in that way."

I let my head tilt to the side. "What do you mean?"

"You're so good, Jamie. You're just wonderful, and I don't want your job to make anybody, me especially, think of you any differently. I know that you are a good person. One of the best. I cannot watch you perform an execution, though. It hurts."

My stomach clenched again, the way it had when we first met. I felt briefly lightheaded, like I had been holding my breath for too long.

"I'm not that good a person," I protested quietly. "You shouldn't think that I am."

"But I do. It isn't something that I need to think about. You just are."

My mouth went dry, and I felt myself flush. I looked down at my lap, brushing a bit of dirt off of my trousers.

"Thank you," I said in a low voice, though I was honestly a bit embarrassed.

She laughed and waved me off, but made no move to get back to her cleaning. I bit the inside of my lip.

"You're good, too. I think that there is nobody better in the world. You're just perfect, Eleanor."

I had not meant to say all of what I had. What was it about Eleanor that made me say things without thinking? Why did she make my chest ache and my stomach plummet? She scooted closer and leaned in a little, poking jokingly at my shoulder.

"*You* are perfect."

"I'm really not."

"You're perfect for me," she said, voice nearly a whisper.

"Have you ever been in love?" I asked suddenly, watching her as she watched me. Was that what this was? Love?

Her eyes widened and she pulled away a little, then laughed and leaned back in. "I think I have."

"I think I have, too."

"Do you?"

"I think that I might be in love right now."

"I might be, as well," she said. Her voice was teasing, but her eyes were serious.

"Do you want to tell me who you might be in love with?" I asked, heart pounding in my ears.

She considered it, screwing up her face and leaning back.

"I suppose I could give you a hint."

She inched closer, slowly, and it felt as if we were falling into each other, like the stars were aligning and the moon was changing, like it was meant to happen, bound to be, sooner or later, for better or for worse.

## TWELVE

All of a sudden, her lips were on mine.

They were soft, and they were full, and they felt like they belonged there, between my own.

*What is happening?*

I nearly could not bring myself to care.

Leaning in a little, I pressed my nose to hers, felt the bump on its bridge, and let my fingers trail to her waist. Her hands moved to find my cheeks, one in each hand, and one of her fingers tangled itself in my hair. I did not want to let go, not at all, but I knew that I would have to at some point.

I pulled back slowly, letting what I had just done register in my brain. Her eyes opened and focused on my face, her lips falling closed and blood rushing into her cheeks.

"I'm so sorry, I—" she shook her head and I

shook mine, raising my hands. "I didn't mean to."

She definitely had meant to, but so had I, and I didn't want to admit it, either.

"That's alright. Everything is alright... I'm just going to leave now," I said hurriedly, hopping down from the haystack and making my way to the barn door.

"Jamie, I'm sorry!" Eleanor called, her voice breaking slightly.

"Don't worry about it!" I yelled back. Briefly, I hoped that I was dreaming. At the same time, I did not want to be dreaming, in case I woke up and forgot all of it. I also hoped, for a moment, that she would follow me up the road, but I quickly discarded that thought. I had never been kissed before, I realized on my way home. At twenty-three, I probably should have had that experience. Eleanor must have been kissed before. Surely, she would know what to do and how to act.

I did not. Not at all.

Nearly tripping over a shrew that was running across the road, I crossed and ran the rest of the way home. When I arrived, my thighs were burning, and my lungs were heaving. I shut the door with a *bang* and fell back against it, one hand on the doorknob and the other on my chest.

*What was that?*

I forced myself to let go of the doorknob, the hand that had been there making its way up to my lips, lingering in the spots where I felt as though Eleanor's lips had left markings, something permanent and golden, declarations of what we had done.

I kicked my heel against the door and threw my head back, letting it knock against the wood as I sighed and looked around the house. Nothing had changed since I had been kissed. Not even though I had been kissed by a woman. Nothing.

Nothing except for the fact that, now, I knew that I might want to be more than Eleanor's friend.

I might love Eleanor Collins, and she might love me, too.

\*\*\*

I was finishing the gardening that I had started two days before, when Eleanor showed up, not bothering to try the door and instead stepping around the house to meet me in the garden.

"Hi," she greeted quietly, hands behind her back, head down. She had pulled her hair back into a long braid that ran down her spine, tied with a dark blue ribbon at the bottom.

"Hello," I said. I didn't meet her eyes. I wondered which of us would be the first to break the silence or to apologize. Though, I suddenly thought we had not done anything worth apologizing for.

Eleanor smoothed out her skirt with her hands. I felt her eyes wander over me before she took a seat in front of me, kneeling in the grass and effectively soaking her knees.

"You're going to get your skirt all muddy," I warned.

"I don't care. My knees are already wet."

"Alright."

We were quiet again for a moment while I covered a group of seeds in the soil from the pile beside me. It had begun to drizzle. I brushed my bangs away from my eyes and felt the mud from my hands leave a sticky mark on my forehead.

"I really am sorry about earlier," Eleanor said finally. "I shouldn't have done what I did."

I wiped my hands off on my trousers and cleaned the mud from my face. "You have nothing to apologize for. I didn't mind it at all."

"Then why are things different between us now?" she asked with an anxious laugh. "Nothing has to be different, does it?"

I sighed. "I'm not sure that things can go back to normal straight away after two friends have kissed."

"But they can eventually, can't they?"

I met her eyes for the first time, watching her pupils dart back and forth from my eyes to my lips and back again. I almost hated that mine were doing the same.

"I think," I said, "that I did not realize how fond I was of you until you kissed me. I did not know that I could feel that way at all. And now that I know that this feeling is somewhat mutual, I'm not sure what to do with myself."

"That's alright," Eleanor reached for my hand. I placed mine in hers, but mine was covered in drying soil and her nails were varnished, and we were both beginning to shiver from the rain. "I'll be right here when you do know."

"That's the worst bit. I know what I would like to do. I would like to take you out for dinner, and I would like to hold your hand in the streets like wives and husbands do." I mumbled. "That's the problem. I know what I would like to do, but it's not about that. I can't have it."

"We can't exactly do those things the way that everybody else can, can we?" she said with a smile, but her eyes were wide and sad.

"I think that is why I've been so confused," I admitted.

"Perhaps," Eleanor said. "People like us can't be too open about it. Not right now, at least."

"I wish that we could. I wish it so much."

"I do, too," she whispered, brushing a strand of hair behind my ear and scrunching up her eyebrows.

"We could keep it a secret," I suggested. "It is an awfully big secret, but nobody needs to know."

Eleanor grinned. "I think that I would like to be with you no matter what, Jamie."

"I think I would like that, too," I told her.

She drew me close to her and I inhaled, wrapping my arms around her and breathing in her perfume and the wool of her coat. Her fingers were weaving their way through my hair like they had been earlier, but this time, I relaxed into them. I pressed my lips to her collarbone.

"We should go indoors," I said into her chest. "We'll freeze out here."

\*\*\*

We played chess with my grandmother's old chess set until sometime around nine o'clock when it grew dark enough that we had to light a candlestick and abandoned our third game in favor of trading funny stories. Eleanor lay across the sofa while I sat cross-legged on the floor in front of the coffee table.

"Are you hungry?" I asked.

"A little," she said, tossing the pawn in her hand up into the air and catching it.

"I can make soup if you would like."

"Or, you could show *me* how to make soup."

"I could do that, too."

We got up and went to the kitchen, Eleanor trailing behind me while I looked for ingredients. She boiled the water while I chopped vegetables.

"I haven't had a good soup in ages," she mused, coughing as steam began to build up. I laughed and moved my pile of chopped broccoli to the side of the cutting board.

"My grandmother taught me how to make it perfectly. Well, she taught me how to make several perfect soups, but potato soup is my favorite."

While I poured the vegetables and cheese into the pot, Eleanor stood behind me, one arm around my shoulder, spoon in hand. She was just a bit taller than me, I noticed when she leaned down a bit to kiss my cheek.

"Stir," I laughed, shaking her off.

She obeyed, stirring the soup with the most intensity I had ever seen soup be stirred with. I dipped my pinky finger into the pot and tasted it, nodding.

"Try some, Eleanor," I suggested, nudging her. She did and smiled.

"How did you manage to make it taste so good? I don't even normally like broccoli."

"It's the seasonings. I add more cayenne than most people do. A lot of people usually add too little, I think. Seasonings can make or break a soup."

We spooned it into two large bowls, though Eleanor made it very clear that, yes, she would be perfectly fine eating it straight from the pot, and poured up two glasses of water before sitting together at the kitchen table with a candle blazing between us. All too often, it seemed, I ate alone. It was nice to have somebody with me for a change, especially when it was her.

"This is nice," Eleanor commented as she picked up a spoonful. "Bad cooking might have been a dealbreaker."

"Well, I'm grateful for my cookbooks, then," I replied.

She set her spoon down and rested her chin in her hand, watching me with a smile as I finished eating.

"What are you doing?" I grinned before taking a drink.

"Just looking. You're very pretty."

I scoffed, but said, "So are you."

She shook her head, still smiling. Once we had finished, we washed the dishes together and I brought her to my bedroom.

"You can stay the night, if you would like to. It's too dark for you to walk home alone, now."

She accepted one of my nightgowns and changed into it while I went around the house, checking that I had blown out all of my candles and turned off the stove. Once I had finished, I laid down in bed and Eleanor sprawled off next to me, stretched out like a cat. One hand held her head up and the other was in mine, rubbing circles on my palm with her thumb.

"I wish that I could tell everybody about us, Jamie," she said quietly, like she was ashamed to say it. It was similar to what she had told me earlier.

"You will, someday," I assured, but I knew it was a lie. She did, too.

She curled up against me and let me hook one leg around hers. I closed my eyes and looked down at her until she fell asleep with my fingers running through her curls, my arms around her body, feeling her chest rise and fall against mine. It occurred to me, before I drifted off, that I would have been content to fall asleep this way every night, wrapped around Eleanor and bathed in silver moonlight.

Nobody visited me that night. The cornfield stayed a cornfield, the moon stayed the moon, and the dead stayed dead. Eleanor and I stayed Eleanor and I, and we slept uninterrupted.

## THIRTEEN

I woke to the cool morning air brushing my sleeveless shoulders. Eleanor was tucked into the crook of my arm, pressed up against my side. Her hair was tangled from the pillowcase, her cheeks flushed and her lips pink. Her face was peaceful, a sort of peacefulness that I didn't think I had ever seen her wear, one that only came in sleep. Often, I assumed, the peaceful air that she had surrounded herself with was one that she feigned, one that came from a lifetime of practice. This was different.

I wrapped the bed sheets further around my shoulders and pressed a kiss to Eleanor's forehead. Her eyebrows pinched and the bridge of her nose wrinkled, and she opened her eyes to look up at me.

"Good morning," I whispered.

"Good morning. Your house is positively freezing."

I hummed in agreement and twirled a strand of her hair around my finger. She sighed contentedly and smiled.

"How did you sleep?" she asked.

"Wonderfully," I said truthfully. It was a relief to say it aloud, to confirm that I hadn't woken up once. I had hardly slept a full night since taking the job, barely one night without seeing people outside of the house or waking in a cold sweat, plagued with nightmares and endless guilt.

"That's good, then. I was half-afraid that I would wake at some point with an axe murderer standing over me," she joked. I knew it was a joke, and it didn't sting the way that it might have if a stranger had said it, somebody other than her.

"I would have fought them off," I laughed, and she pretended to swoon.

"Would you?"

"Yes. Nobody would have hurt you."

She rolled her eyes but lifted a hand to rest it on my cheek, circling her thumb back and forth on my cheekbone. I reached up and caught the hand in my own.

"We could run away together," she suggested.

I snorted. "We could try."

"I'm serious, Jamie. You're unhappy here, and I'm barely doing anything. We should just leave, should we not? My Aunt Clara's cabin in Indiana has been empty for four years now, and she left it for me when she died."

I pulled back. "Why have you not gone to live there already, then?"

"I don't know..." she sighed. "I loved my job. That kept me here. Since losing it, I've just been thinking about somehow getting it back. I think that now, I know that it's not going to happen. I'm ready to have a different dream."

"Really?"

She nodded, rolling over to face me completely. "Really."

"Just—" I shook my head with a smile, blushing and slightly overwhelmed. "Give me some time to think about it. Alright?"

"Of course. I don't want you to feel pressured into this at all," she said. "Just let me know when you find your answer."

\*\*\*

We walked to the barn together after having a breakfast of jam on toast and tea. Eleanor had wanted to try planting some dahlias, and I knew that Atticus' daughter, Helena, still had some leftover from the spring.

Eleanor was wearing my jumper and the skirt that she had worn the day before. My grandmother had knit the jumper that she was wearing, and it was nice to see somebody else wearing it other than myself.

When we arrived, Atticus was pacing back and forth, running one hand up and down his beard and pulling at his hair with the other while he muttered furiously under his breath.

"Mr. Jones?" I said.

"Did the onion vendor at the market finally sell more than Florence?" Eleanor grinned.

"Actually, Eleanor," Atticus spun around to face her, glaring between the two of us with blazing eyes. "This involves you and your *husband*."

I dropped her hand, which I had been holding behind my back, and stared at her. Her smile dropped rapidly, the color draining from her face in an instant.

"Your what?" I asked quietly.

Eleanor swallowed audibly and tears began to gather at the corners of her eyes as her breathing quickened and her cheeks flushed.

"You have got no right to stand there and act as if you know what happened between us. He is not my husband anymore."

"Well," Atticus snarled, "he certainly seems to think that he is. In fact, he wants you good and dead."

My head snapped from Eleanor to Atticus, ears ringing. "What is going on?"

"He," Eleanor said quietly, speaking through clenched teeth, "is dead."

"You're married?" I asked.

"Not anymore. He's dead."

"That doesn't mean that you aren't married!"

Atticus stepped in, thrusting a large finger in Eleanor's face. She flinched as he did so, and her already trembling body grew more tense. I wasn't entirely sure, at that moment, whether I was angrier with Eleanor for not telling me about her marriage, or with Atticus for upsetting her.

"Hugh Clayton wants you dead, and he says that it's because you tried to kill him."

"I had to," Eleanor choked out, at the same time that I said, "You tried to kill him?"

Atticus folded his arms across his chest. "Is it true?"

Eleanor opened her mouth, closed it, and looked down at her feet, before settling for nodding.

My stomach sank. "Why did you have to, Eleanor?"

Atticus took a step back, running his hands

through his hair. He took a deep breath and shook his head. "I can't just keep you hidden, Collins. It's bad enough that I've had you working for me. I have to tell the sheriff, and you will have to die."

Eleanor slumped down into a heap on the ground and buried her face in her hands. "He's in town?"

"He sure as hell is."

"He'll just kill me himself."

Atticus scoffed. "I never would have pegged you as a madwoman. You seemed too soft."

"I *had* to!" she yelled tearfully. "He would have killed me first if I hadn't!"

Atticus slammed his fist against the wall and Eleanor jumped. He turned and stormed out of the barn, heavy footfalls fading as he disappeared.

I sat down next to her and sighed, turning to face her. "Why did you do it? Why did you not tell me?"

She lifted her head and met my eyes. "He hurt me."

"Yes, I understand that," I huffed. "I'm still confused, though."

"I needed to leave, but he told me that I couldn't get away without being hurt worse," she shuddered. "I only did it because I had to."

"When?"

"I met him when I was… sixteen, probably. Yes. I was sixteen years old. He was eighteen."

When she didn't go on, I nudged her knee with my own. She shrugged. "I had never been loved before, Jamie. I thought it was *supposed* to be suffocating."

"When did you try to kill him, though?"

"I hit him over the back of the head with a pipe on my eighteenth birthday while he was gathering firewood."

My mouth fell open, and I stared at her. "Oh. Alright."

"That was the same day that Joseph and I moved here," she explained, inhaling deeply. "I assumed that he had bled out and died."

We were quiet for a while before I said, "It took him long enough to tell somebody. I suppose he left out all of what he did, though."

"He might have been in a coma. Might have been with his parents. He could have been up to anything," she huffed. "He wasn't the one who had to hide."

"Stupid twat."

She laughed breathily; eyes wet. "I'm sorry."

"I wish you wouldn't apologize, Eleanor."

"I didn't tell you that I was married. I was trying to keep it all in the past."

"Yes, well, you thought it was the right thing to do, I suppose," I said.

She nodded. "Sometimes I feel like... perhaps, if I don't think about it, I'll forget it."

"That's nothing to be sorry about. I just wish that I could have done something to help. I wish that I could still do something."

"I don't..." she took a deep breath and leaned forward, setting her shoulders. "This sort of thing is not easy to fix."

I took her hands and waited for her to look at me. It took a moment, but she met my eyes all the same.

"You can speak to me, Eleanor. I know that it won't fix anything, but I can always listen."

Eleanor brought my hand to her lips. "Thank you."

*\*\*\**

Eleanor stayed with me again that night. We spent the evening speaking about what we would do in Indiana if we did move, how we would get there, when we would go. It was comforting, in a way, to know that I had somebody to lean on and somewhere to go if being alone in Kansas ever became too much.

*You aren't alone anymore*, I reminded myself. It

was a thought that was almost foreign, but it was nice. Still, as much as I tried to focus on the future, on our life, I couldn't seem to stop myself from worrying about Hugh. I probably should have asked more questions about Eleanor or found out a little bit more about her marriage, but I could not possibly bring myself to do that. Surely, Eleanor would not want to live that again, and I would not want her to have to, just for my own sake.

Curled up in bed at ten o'clock that night in a white nightgown, Eleanor squeezed my hand twice.

"I'm a little worried," she admitted in a small voice. I drew away.

"Why?" I asked, knowing it was a stupid question.

"What if he finds us? I've been so careless since leaving him. I really thought that he was dead. What if he knows where we are?" she drew a shaky breath. "What if he finds Joseph?"

"Stay with me. You can write to Joseph every day if it will make you feel better. You can live here with me, and you'll have no reason to worry. I will answer the door from now on, or the door will stay locked. Whatever will make you feel safe."

She looked up at me, sniffling. "I must sound silly, complaining about this when you feel this scared all of the time."

"You don't sound silly at all. You don't have to diminish your feelings just because of me," I chided. "I've just learned to bear it."

"I'm not sure if I can bear it," she laughed humorlessly. "I've done that for so long."

"Then let me bear it for you."

Eleanor bit her bottom lip. Her teeth left an indentation. "I can't ask you to do that. I don't want you to have to worry about me all of the time."

"I don't have to do anything, Eleanor. I'll do it because I love you."

She looked up at me, eyes wide and round. "Are we rushing into this?"

I had asked myself the same question just the night before and dismissed it just as quickly. I shook my head. "No... Do you think so?"

"I think that I love you very much. But, I don't want you to regret all of this someday."

"Never."

"Well, then, I'll stay with you. I want you to let me know if there is anything that I can do to help out, though," she said.

I smiled. "Yes, yes. Now, go to sleep."

She rolled back onto her side and closed her eyes. While she dozed off, I stayed awake and stared up at the ceiling for hours.

When I finally did shut my eyes, I couldn't help thinking that this was all the more reason to get out of Kansas.

## FOURTEEN

The final execution was unexpected. While Eleanor was still asleep, I walked back to the barn to get the dahlia seeds that I had meant to get the day before. Upon my arrival, Atticus pulled me into the barn and looked at me thoughtfully.

"We need an execution done right away. As soon as possible. Now, preferably."

It took me a moment to process what he had said. I stared at him, open-mouthed, and stuttered out a "No."

"Oh, Foster. One last go, and then you're off the hook. This man is wanted for murder, and we can't just let him out and about."

"I'll give you something to think about," I said. "How about we find Hugh Clayton and kill him instead?"

Atticus folded his arms over his chest. "How about you do what you're told? Don't think I won't tell the sheriff about Eleanor if you don't do this."

"You're insane. Forcing me to do this by threatening my best friend? That's awful, Jones."

"Are you going to perform the execution, or not?"

I agreed to do it, under the condition that I get paid double.

\*\*\*

The man's name was Jon. He had been arrested and charged with the murder of a carpenter, his co-worker, who had received the promotion that Jon had been working to earn. I wanted to finish the execution as quickly as possible, hoping that if it were quick, and I kept my eyes shut, I would not take in a thing, and he would not come to haunt me in the middle of the night.

When I arrived back home, the house was silent and empty. My footsteps echoed through the hallway as I made my way to the bedroom, the sound of my own breathing bouncing off the walls. In the bedroom, I rifled through the drawer of my nightstand until I found the letter of resignation buried beneath several boxes of matchsticks. I stuffed it deep into the pocket of my coat and left the room.

Eventually, I found Eleanor sitting in the garden, digging at the ground with one of my spades. Her hair was tied back into a ponytail, and she wore a pair of my old trousers.

"Hi," I said. "I brought the seeds."

She stopped digging and looked up at me with a smile. "That's perfect! Are we going to start today? I've already started digging a hole, and—"

"We might have to wait for a bit," I interrupted, avoiding her eyes. "We're out of vegetables. And bread. So, I'll have to go back to the market now."

"That's alright. We can plant these when you get back, right?"

"Right." I shoved the seeds in her direction and turned around quickly, one hand in my coat pocket to be sure that I had my letter.

"Are you leaving again, now?" Eleanor called as I opened the door.

"Yes, but I'll be home soon," I assured. "You can start planting the seeds while you wait for me, if you would like to."

She shook her head and stood, attempting unsuccessfully to brush the dirt from her pants. "It will be nice for us to do it together. I can wait."

"Alright. I'll be back soon," I repeated. She grabbed my cheek with the heel of her hand, in an attempt to avoid brushing her mud-covered fingers against my face, and pressed a kiss to my forehead. I kissed her nose and waved her goodbye, then made my way back to the barn.

*****

I performed the execution just two hours later, after spending the rest of the afternoon wandering around the market. I knew that Eleanor would be suspicious, after I had been gone so long, but I hoped that she would forgive me. We only had to get through tonight.

"Ladies and gentlemen," Atticus boomed as I pulled on my robes that evening. "This, *I regret to inform you* all, might be our last execution."

I wrinkled my nose. There were noises of protest from the crowd, patches of silence, and sighs of what might have been relief or disappointment. I replayed Atticus' words.

I regret to inform you.

I wondered how he managed to care so little about it all.

Jon was a short man with a thick neck and a head of blond hair, cut into the shape of a mushroom cap. His eyes were beady, like a rat's, and his nose was small. I eyed him carefully as he flexed his hands, uninterested as Atticus spoke. He seemed not to care about what was coming, like he had known when he had killed his coworker that he, too, would die, and that he was not sorry in the least.

Once Atticus had concluded his speech, I stepped up onto the concrete block and let Jon get to his knees. I waited for him to lay his head against the wooden block. He knelt, but all he did was look up at me. I looked back.

"Please lay your head on the wooden block, sir," I instructed. It felt insensitive and inhumane, and a shiver shot down my spine.

"Yes, ma'am," he said, but his voice was mocking as he did as he was told.

I looked out into the crowd of people, examining the faces of the onlookers, watching as Peter eyed my sword, his face disgusted, tinted with interest. He seemed not to recognize me, like he was looking at somebody whom he had never met. I noticed William's mother standing toward the back, one hand resting upon her chest and eyes cast down. This was the last time, I reminded myself, that I would do this. The money would not matter after today. I would get a new job in Indiana.

"Forgive me," I said, cringing as it came out louder than I had intended. Jon twisted around to look me in the eyes.

"I already have."

My stomach clenched and I raised my arms, the sword weighing them down, muscles protesting. The sword was heavy, but it also felt familiar, and I wondered if this was anything like how King Arthur felt, if his arms shook, if his chest tightened.

I squeezed my eyes shut and turned my head away, ensuring that I would not have to watch as I brought the sword down.

It did not go as smoothly as the others had, however, and I let out a pained breath when the sword connected with something that was definitely not wood. I opened my eyes reluctantly to see what had happened.

Jon's head had not been entirely severed, still clinging desperately to his body.

"Try it again!" somebody shouted from the front of the crowd. I swallowed with difficulty and cringed, lifting the sword and bringing it down once more, successfully decapitating Jon. I was then left standing beside his limp, mangled body, watching his blood stain the block, dripping onto the dead and dying grass beneath me, the sword coated. It had splattered onto my shoes, as well, and all that I could smell was the metallic scent. It seemed as if there was more blood around me today than I had ever seen in my entire life.

I ran from the block to the barn, pulling my

robes off on the way and thrusting them into the corner, where I also tossed my sword. It made a loud clatter when it hit the wooden floorboards, a sound like thunder. I would never wear those robes again, never hold the sword again, which should have been comforting, but all that I could think about was the blood and the sight of Jon's half-decapitated body, the cries of disgust and horror from the crowd, the absence of feeling from Atticus.

He walked into the barn, clapping me on the shoulder. "I'm glad that you didn't back down, Foster."

I pulled my letter of resignation from my coat pocket and handed it to him. "I want the check now, please. Then you'll never see me again."

Atticus rolled his eyes, pulling his miniature checkbook from his back pocket and carelessly tearing a sheet from it. "Oh, please, enough with the dramatics. I gave you a wonderful opportunity with this job, and you wasted it."

I grabbed the check from his hand after he scribbled his signature furiously and turned on my heel, before pausing in the doorway.

"You feel no remorse for this, do you?" I said.

"These people are criminals."

I left before he could say anything more and

stared at the four-figured number on the slip of paper in my hand all the way home.

Had any of this been worth the money?

\*\*\*

"Where have you been?" Eleanor called from the kitchen, sounding more worried than angry. Understandably. I had been out for far too long for somebody who had claimed to be buying salt and pepper.

She was sitting at the table, a deck of playing cards stacked neatly in front of her and a teacup to her right. Her hair was down, and she had a hand to her mouth as if she had been biting at her nails.

I locked the door behind me and stumbled into the kitchen, collapsing into the chair across from her and covering my face with my hands as I finally let myself cry.

"Jamie," Eleanor said, making her way to my chair and crouching in front of me. "What happened?"

"I just killed somebody else," I gasped.

"What?"

"His head…" I kicked the leg of the table and sobbed. Eleanor touched the toe of my shoe where Jon's blood had stained. "His head wouldn't even come off. Stupid, thick neck. I had to do it *twice*."

Eleanor winced and turned away, one hand coming to rest on my thigh and the other curled into a fist, pressed to her lips. "Did you know that you would have to do this when you left earlier?"

I hesitated but nodded slowly. "He told me when I went to get the seeds."

"Why did you not tell me?" she asked softly.

I slammed the check onto the table. Eleanor flinched. "He told me that he would tell the sheriff about you and Hugh if I didn't."

Eleanor's jaw clenched, but she sat down cross-legged and took my hands.

"You need to breathe, Jamie," she said.

I inhaled deeply and dropped my forehead onto her shoulder, letting her run her fingers through my hair as I closed my eyes and steadied my breathing.

"I don't want to do *this* anymore," I sighed.

"Then quit, love."

"I already did. I mean, I don't want to do this. I want to leave. Let's just leave. Please."

She wrapped her arms around me, squeezing tightly. I was sure that, though I had never been so horrified in my life, I had also never felt as safe as I did in her arms.

"Are you absolutely sure?" she asked. "You can sleep on it."

"No, I want to," I pressed.

"Well, we can leave tomorrow, if you would like to. We can walk to my house, take my car, and go from there."

I nodded and pressed a kiss to Eleanor's cheek. We would be alright. I knew that we would be, eventually. We just had to make it through the night.

*****

I woke with my arms around Eleanor's waist, shivering from the cold. Squinting at the pocket watch on my nightstand, I sat up and looked around.

Three o'clock in the morning was never a good time to be awake, especially when you have just killed somebody. A stray dog was barking in the distance and Eleanor stirred lightly next to me, stretching out on the mattress and reaching for my hand.

"Eleanor," I whispered.

"Yes, Jamie?"

"I think that they're back."

"Who is back?"

I got up and peeked through the curtains, shocked when nobody looked back at me from the cornfield. "The visions, or whatever you called them."

Eleanor joined me at the window and rested her hands on my shoulders, pushing me down into the chair at my desk. "It's alright. Look, you're safe with me, right?"

I shook my head. "No, Eleanor, they're here. They're somewhere. You don't understand. I cannot deal with seeing the man who I killed today."

"Take a deep breath and we can go back to sleep, then."

I stood again, ignoring her, and made my way to the bathroom. Eleanor followed me, hair tangled and cheeks red as she looked around. She followed me to the living room and then to the kitchen, where I froze and gasped.

William, Francis, Anne and Jon were standing outside of the window. I shrieked when I saw Jon, his head hanging from his body, blood running down his neck and pooling in a puddle on the ground. I turned around and pressed the heels of my hands into my eyes until I saw stars.

"Are they here?" Eleanor asked, taking a step closer to the window.

"They're all outdoors. His head is hanging, and he's bleeding everywhere."

Eleanor shuddered. "What do we do?"

"I'm not sure, but I don't want to look again."

"Alright. Keep your eyes shut while I close the curtains."

I could not keep my eyes shut. I turned back to the window despite myself, watching in horror as they all, simultaneously, walked toward the house. Eleanor drew the curtains closed and they stopped in their tracks, their silhouettes and the whites of their eyes still visible through the curtains, though just barely so.

"There," she said.

"Their eyes," I tried to explain. "I can still see them."

She guided me down to sit on the tiled floor and knelt behind me. I reached around to grasp at her hand, but both of her hands came to settle over my eyes, shielding me from anything around me. I sighed, relieved, and wiped at my cheeks. After what could have been five minutes or could have been an hour, I turned around to face Eleanor.

"I don't want to see them anymore," I said tiredly. I stood and let her lead me back to the bedroom. "They aren't gone for good, Eleanor."

She kissed the back of my hand.

"I know, Jamie. But, look around. They aren't here anymore. I'm here."

"You're here."

"I am."

"And they're gone for now."

"They are."

I sighed. "They aren't here."

"Not at all."

"Alright."

Breathless and lightheaded, I laid back down and waited for Eleanor to settle next to me. Before, I had been the one with my arms around her at night, holding onto her like a lifeline, like a child holding their teddy bear, how I had often seen my father hold my mother. Tonight, however, she wrapped her arms around me and let me close my eyes first, letting me believe that everything would be alright if she was there with me.

"We'll be away from here soon enough."

## FIFTEEN

I locked the front door and stood on the front porch to stare through the window, into the doorway of my house. Everything that I had wanted to take with me was packed up into three bags and strapped to the top of Eleanor's car. I looked around to make sure that nobody was near before kissing three of my fingers and pressing them to the doorknob.

Leaving was bittersweet. As badly as I wanted to leave, the house had also been my grandmother's. It was where I had spent the majority of my childhood, where I had experienced the things that had shaped me up to this point and where I had formed most of my memories, both good and bad. I felt as if I were saying goodbye to my family all over again.

I knew that I would miss it, but I also knew that Eleanor would not mind driving back to see the house now and again. I would miss the garden, the one that I had worked so hard to keep alive with my grandmother. I would miss the stovetops and their mysterious stains, the rust on the cabinet's hinges, the broken bed springs, and the ratty scarecrow in the cornfield, though I would not miss the cornfield itself one bit.

Indiana would be new for both of us, I reminded myself. It would not be easy for me, nor would it be easy for Eleanor. Although it might not be easy, I knew that it would be worth it.

I was worried about a plethora of things, and Eleanor probably was as well. We had both considered that Hugh very well might make his way up to Indiana at some point. The day before, I had expressed my worries about leaving my house unattended. Eleanor had mentioned that she was worried about finding work. I was, too, I had said, but we would cross these bridges when we came to them.

She strapped the last of the bags to the top of the car as I came to sit in the passenger seat and waited for her as she cranked the car. The car was small and had clearly been bought second-hand, though it was possibly second-hand before that. It was boxy and, though the paint was peeling terribly, might have once been the color of a red apple. It was faded and rusted, now.

Once she had finished, Eleanor fell into the driver's seat and brushed the hair out of her eyes before placing both hands lazily on the wheel. She turned to face me.

"Are you absolutely sure about this?" she asked, searching my eyes for any signs of hesitation.

"One hundred percent," I confirmed.

"It's alright if you aren't, you know. We could always just call it quits and stay right here. I don't—" she faltered as I grasped her face between my palms, effectively cutting her off.

"I want to do this," I said as I dropped one hand and let the other linger on her cheek. "I promise. I do."

I had expected her to continue rambling, to tell me that we could have a life together in Kansas, that it would be alright to call it off, that perhaps we were not entirely ready for all of this. But, instead, she took my hand from her cheek and laced her fingers through mine, squeezing softly and letting out a breath.

"Last chance."

"Eleanor."

"Jamie."

"Drive."

So, she drove.

\*\*\*

Halfway to Indiana, when the sky had turned inky and black, we came to a stop in front of a red house with rose bushes around the driveway. The roof was in serious need of repairs, and the paint on the house was splotchy, obviously having just recently covered up another color. But the greenery around the house certainly made up for it. Eleanor removed her hands from the steering wheel and leaned forward to get a good look at the house, eyeing it up and down skeptically.

"Where are we?" I asked.

"My brother's house."

"Are you going to go inside?"

"I haven't decided yet," she said, sitting back and pursing her lips. "His house is rather ugly now that he's painted it."

I laughed, surprised, and put my hands over hers.

"You seem nervous," I observed.

"I just hate worrying him. And I know that he will worry. Maybe I'll leave it for now," she began to fiddle with her necklace.

"You probably should go see him, Eleanor," I

argued lightly. "Just so that he knows where you are, if nothing else."

Eleanor sighed and nodded. "I suppose so."

I shot her an encouraging smile and she smiled back. I leaned over and pushed her door open.

"Go," I urged. She rolled her eyes, but her smile didn't fall as she stepped out of the car and walked to the front door, knocking with two knuckles in the light way that she did. I watched through the car window as she stood in the cold, enveloped in foggy night air while she waited for Joseph to open the door. She turned around to face me and mouthed something that I barely caught: *he isn't home.*

But there were lights on at the back of the house and a car in the driveway that stated otherwise, and a moment later, the door swung open, and a tall, slender young man with long, unruly brown curls and dark eyes like Eleanor's emerged, leaning on a cane. He was wearing his pajamas, a confused expression on his face.

Eleanor said something to him, and he stepped forward to wrap her in a hug, bending down to kiss her head. It was funny, how he looked so much older than her, though I knew that he was younger. She reached up to wrap her arms around his neck, and they stayed like this for a long moment until Eleanor pulled away and told him something else. He shook his head and, though I tried to read his lips, I couldn't tell what Joseph was saying to her. Part of me thought that I should look away, that this might be a moment that I should not be present for, but I couldn't bring myself to do that. I had never felt the love of a sibling or been particularly close to any of my cousins. This kind of love seemed so foreign and beautiful.

When Joseph finally shut the door, Eleanor stood on his front step for a moment longer before turning around and wiping her eyes. She made her way back to the car slowly, opening the door without a word and turning to look at me with a smile.

"Is everything alright?" I asked.

"Everything is perfect."

We drove for two more hours and fell asleep on the dead end of an old dirt road, just the two of us cramped up in the front of Eleanor's car with my head in her lap and her hands in my hair.

\*\*\*

When Eleanor nudged me awake, we were sitting in front of a log cabin surrounded by trees. There was an ivy-covered birdbath at the end of the driveway and an empty flower box by the front door. I realized, suddenly, that this was it. This could be our oasis.

"This is it," she sighed, echoing my thoughts with her eyes closed and head against the headrest. She said it as if it were a miracle that we had made it, had been a fear that we might not. I grinned and opened the door. It was light out now, and there was a blanket of mist settling around us, preparing to become fog.

"Do we have any neighbors?" I asked when I got out.

"I think so," Eleanor said, sparing a glance to the large, white cabin to the right of us where a truck was parked in the rocky driveway. There was trim on the roof and large windows at the front of the house, rose bushes in the garden, and a bird-house hanging from a branch on one of the trees. It looked exactly like a house from a storybook.

Smiling, Eleanor went around the car and began to unload our bags.

"Leave that alone," I said. "I'll get this. You go inside and see what it's like."

She kissed my cheek and thanked me before rolling out her shoulders and opening the front door. I caught a quick glimpse of the kitchen and smiled even wider. We would cook in that kitchen soon enough, I thought. We could make endless soup—we could make whatever we wanted. We could make endless bread, endless casseroles, chop thousands of vegetables and get an old brown dog and a black kitten to keep as pets.

I brought our bags inside and set them on the floor, plopping down onto the couch next to Eleanor and stretching my legs out.

"We might need to do some touching up," she admitted, looking around at the peeling wallpaper and the cobwebs in the corners of the ceiling.

"We can worry about all of that later."

"I should go to the market. I passed one down the road, and we've got no food."

"You've been driving for hours, Eleanor," I said.

"Do you fancy starving, Jamie?"

"I'll go, if it will settle you any," I offered.

"Thank you."

I got back to my feet and went outside again, walking down the road in the cool afternoon air to the market. It was easy enough to find, with large stands and handwritten wooden signs.

The first vendor who caught my eye was a man who looked eerily similar to Peter, with dark brown skin and a mustache, tight curls, and dark eyes.

"Hello," I greeted. He gave me a smile and greeted me right back, and it puzzled me how much he even spoke like Peter. Then, he leaned his elbows on the table and stood, silently, and watched as I rooted through his bread to find the best loaf that I could.

"You must be new here, ma'am," he finally commented as I worked my way through his vegetables.

"Why do you say that?" I asked, looking up at him with two peppers in my hand.

"Everybody knows everybody here. I think it odd that I have yet to meet you."

I laid an armful of vegetables and a loaf of bread on his table and dug around my pocket to fish out my money.

"We just moved into that log cabin up there," I said as I pointed to it, picturing Eleanor watching us through the kitchen window.

"That cabin has been empty for years," he sighed, taking my coins and counting them out. "It will be nice to finally have somebody living there again. All of us miss Clara a whole lot."

"Clara's niece is living in that cabin with me now, sir. We just came here from Kansas."

The man nodded along. "You should take a visit to the family next door. They've been looking for a nanny since Clara died. Mention it to her niece, would you, Miss?"

I reached out to shake his hand and loaded my

groceries into my arms. "I certainly will. Thank you, sir."

"Have a nice day, Jamie!" he called after me as I turned away. I frowned and spun back around.

"Have we met before?" I asked.

"Not that I recall."

"How did you know my name, then? I don't remember giving it to you."

"Ah," it was his turn to frown, scratching his head under the hat which looked a lot like one that Peter had owned when we were children. "That's strange. I could have sworn you had told me."

"Yes, well.... Perhaps I did, then," I said slowly. We parted ways once more, and I decided, as I walked, that Indiana might be fun after all.

***

While we were making tomato soup and tea, Eleanor perched on the countertop with a spoon in one hand and a salt shaker in the other, I brought up the job.

"Have you ever thought about nannying?" I asked. She hummed.

"Of course I have. I do miss children."

"You might be in luck. One of the men at the market told me that a family is living in the cabin next door who have been looking for a nanny since your aunt died."

"Aunt Clara told me that their parents were rich."

"If that were true, they might not be looking up and down for a nanny as they seem to be doing now."

She laughed and dipped a finger in the pot to taste the soup.

"You should speak with them. Maybe they will hire you," I suggested.

"They might need a cook, too," she grinned. I sighed and leaned back against the counter.

"You can ask if you would like to, but I very much doubt that they're looking for both."

"I'm going to ask," Eleanor decided as she handed me a bowl. We poured up the soup and brought it to the table, where our tea, now luke-warm, was waiting.

The table had been covered in a thick layer of dust when we had arrived, and we had needed to sweep it off with an old dishcloth. Eleanor had dug out a moth-eaten tablecloth which was folded up in the hallway closet, and we had laid it down to make the table look a bit nicer.

"I'm very happy that we did this," she said thoughtfully as I set down two spoons.

"I am, too."

Eleanor sat down across from me and rested her chin in her hand.

"I really do hope that I can get the job. It would be nice to be working at something I love again."

"I'm sure you will. I can't see why you would not."

We ate in comfortable silence, and once we had finished, we sat outside to watch the sun set. We could see it surprisingly well from where we were situated, and the golden glow cast lights across me and Eleanor and the cabin behind us.

## SIXTEEN

The next morning, Eleanor and I made a spice cake and put on our best outfits in preparation to meet our neighbors.

"Are you sure that this looks alright?" Eleanor asked as she pulled at the end of her top. She was wearing a green knit set and frilly white socks, and had put a ribbon in her braided hair.

"Yes, Eleanor."

We had gone over this many times, and she had changed twice before settling on the set. I was wearing a pleated floral black skirt and white cardigan, which was the nicest thing I owned at the moment. I ran my hands over my skirt and checked my hair in the bathroom mirror, then made my way back to the bedroom where Eleanor was sitting on the bed and cleaning her shoes, though she had already cleaned them once that morning. I sat on the floor in front of her and touched her knee. She looked up from her shoes and smiled.

"It's going to be alright," I told her. "I promise. No matter what happens, everything will be fine."

"I know. I just really hope that I get this job," she said. "If I don't get it, I'll have to go looking around town, and I'm not even sure what I would do. I could try to start gardening and then I could work at the market, but…" she trailed off as I shook my head and took her hands.

"Stop worrying for now. We said that we would cross these bridges when we came to them, did we not? If you don't get this job, then you don't get it. We can keep looking. It will not be the end of the world."

She sighed and nodded, picking her shoes back up and setting them on the floor. I laced them up for her once she had slipped them on.

"Are you ready?" she asked as I retrieved the cake from the kitchen and followed her out to the front door.

"I am," I said, and laid my hand over hers on the doorknob. We turned it together and swung the door open, then quickly ducked back into the house to kiss before we left.

\*\*\*

Sure enough, Eleanor was hired as a nanny, and, to my surprise, I was hired to be a cook. That night, we lay together in bed, curled up in a moth-eaten patchwork quilt. Eleanor's head was on my chest, and my legs were wrapped around her own. I could feel the pulse in her neck as it beat against my ribs.

"Thank you," I said quietly. I thought that she might have been asleep, that she might not hear me, but she did, and her fingers began to twist around the ends of my hair.

"What for?" she asked.

"For helping me leave. For not leaving me when you could have, when others probably would have. For teaching me everything that I now know about love."

I felt her smile, and she shifted to look up at me, eyes big and round in the dark. The flame of the candle on the windowsill reflected in her irises.

"You know that you don't have to thank me," she chided.

How many times had we told each other that? I was beginning to lose count. Still, I *wanted* to thank her. She would undoubtedly do the same.

"I love you, Eleanor," I said, instead of saying everything else that came to my mind.

"I love you, too, Jamie."

And suddenly, the dark did not feel as dark, and the guilt did not feel as heavy, and the constant, growing ache in my chest ebbed away, replaced with something resembling hope, something that glowed in the blackness of the bedroom, something that I knew to be pure and true adoration. I was certain that my blood was running golden and that my heart, surely, was ten times bigger and shining silver.

All at once, we were both alright. We were both alright, and it was all very good.

# EPILOGUE

I wanted to marry Eleanor. I knew it after the first year that we lived together. However, we both knew that it could not happen.

We made do, living as if we were married, without actually being so. It was nice to imagine, sometimes to say it aloud with each other. Occasionally, we argued as if we had been living together for five or ten years, and made up just as quickly as we had started. Our life together was rather peaceful, sometimes littered with nightmares or stress that we helped each other through.

It was June of the next year when Eleanor and I invited the family next door, the Smiths, and Joseph, over for dinner. We made a large batch of soup and baked bread and made tea, though the bread had burned a little and had to be soaked a bit in the soup to really be edible.

The little girl, Ruby, who Eleanor nannied, was adding large lumps of sugar to her tea, and her brother, Henry, was playing with one of the local stray dogs. This had become tradition, for the stray dogs to wander inside and curl up under the kitchen table or wait by the refrigerator until we fed it, and leave when it was satisfied. Eleanor and I kept a vase of dahlias on the table, and as she stepped over Henry and the dog, she discreetly pulled one out and handed it to me with a grin.

A few moments later, while I was speaking to Ruby about why, no, she should not feed spoonfuls of sugar to the dog even though she thought it might like it, I noticed Eleanor wander off into the hallway near the bathroom, away from the crowd of people, speaking in a hushed voice to Joseph. He had his back against the wall, one arm propped against his cane, his hair pulled back and his shoes polished. She had a hand on his arm while she spoke, and he responded slowly.

"I went to the sheriff about it," I heard him saying.

"Joe, you did not."

"He *needed* to be locked up, Eleanor. He found me. That means that he could have just as easily found you."

When Eleanor sat back down next to me a few minutes later with flushed cheeks, I nudged her with my elbow.

"Is everything alright?" I asked quietly.

"I suppose it could be worse," she sighed, leaning back in her seat. "Hugh found out where Joseph was living back in March and stopped by his house to see if I was living with him. Joseph told him no, and gave him the address of one of the abandoned homes a while away. He reported him to the sheriff."

"Has he been arrested?"

"Yes. He's still in prison."

"This is good, right?"

"Well," she bit her lip and looked around to make sure that everybody was busy, that nobody was listening. Joseph was engaged in a very animated conversation with the Smiths, and the children were feeding bits of their bread to the dog, who was more than happy to eat it. "I just feel like I should be happier about it. I'm glad that he has been arrested and that he can't do to anybody else now what he did to me. But, I don't feel happy or relieved like I think I should. I just feel tired."

"That's to be expected," I said. "Like you said, he can't hurt you or anybody else anymore. You can let all of it go, now. You're safe."

Minding our company, we did not hold each other's hands or exchange a kiss like we might have if we were alone. But, Eleanor shifted closer to me and I pressed my hand to her back for a moment. In the silence, a bird pecked at the window, and Joseph opened it and tossed a piece of bread outside for the bird to eat.

"Did you hear that Peter Pritchett's twin brother works at the market? Mrs. Smith told me last night. He must have moved here *ages* ago," Eleanor mentioned offhandedly, observing the children at the table as they crowded around the dog.

"I think I've met him already. The first day we were here…"

"Miss Eleanor," Henry said suddenly, interrupting us. "Do you have any more bread? The dog has finished mine."

***

The night after our gathering, I sat down at the kitchen table in my nightgown with a stack of papers and a pencil, and I wrote four letters: one to Francis, one to Jon, one to Anne, and one that I was still writing. I wrote about my reasons for seeking out the job, about my guilt and my apologies, but most importantly, I wrote updates on their families from the last I had heard of them and wrote about what was going on in the world. I wanted them to know that they had not been forgotten. Not in the least.

"Jamie," Eleanor called as she made her way down the stairs, rubbing at her eyes with the palm of her hand and coming to meet me at the table. "It's late, love."

"Just a moment," I said, looking up to press a kiss to her jaw. She touched my shoulder and went back upstairs to our bedroom. I looked back down at the paper and then at the envelope, which was addressed to myself, and then back to the paper that I was currently writing on. I contemplated scrapping the whole thing, cringing as I read over what I had already written, reminded why I had not pursued a career as a writer. However, I finished the letter and read it over once more.

*Jamie,*

*Your parents named you Jamie after your grandmother, and your grandmother was not a coward. But, neither are you.*

*I'm sorry that you could not forgive yourself for doing what you thought would help you, and I'm sorry that you did not know how to deal with it or what to do. But mostly, I'm sorry that you did not think that you were worthy or allowed to live the life that you are liv-*

*ing now.*

*You need to learn to let go of things. Eleanor tells you, coming from somebody who has dealt with immense stress since she was a child, that she thinks that your hallucinations stem from stress similar to hers. She thinks that, if you learn to forgive yourself, it might help. You are learning to do that now, and that is why I decided to write to you. Though you might not have always thought so, you are allowed to forgive yourself for the things that you did when you thought that it was your only option.*

*You are loved. You are forgiven. You are more than that, even. Because now, you are peaceful. Everything is alright. You know it's true, because Eleanor told you so.*

*Jamie*

I folded the paper twice and gathered it up with the rest of the letters, then shoved them all into a shoebox in the hallway closet and let my hands linger over it for a while. I pushed the box to the back of the closet and buried it in a pile of towels. Tears gathered in my eyes and I willed myself to keep them at bay. It was odd to think that I could be peaceful. I had lived in chaos for so long that I had nearly forgotten what it meant to feel content.

Closing the closet door slowly so that it would

not squeak, I stepped away and began to make my way upstairs to meet Eleanor.

"Alright?" Eleanor asked sleepily as I pushed back the covers and settled in beside her. I wrapped my arms around her shoulders and let my chin rest on her shoulder as she took my hands.

"Perfect."

\*\*\*

Eleanor and I took care of the children the next night while their parents both worked. She put Ruby to bed and, though I was only the cook, I tucked Henry in. He had taken a strong liking to me, though I could not possibly imagine why. I had never been any good with children. Nevertheless, that night he insisted that I tell him a story.

"What kind of story?" I asked.

He frowned, face pinched in thought. "I want to hear a nice one."

I sat at the foot of the bed and sighed, combing my brain for ideas. I was, as I mentioned, not a writer by any means and conjuring up a story was a challenge.

"You've stumped me there, Hen," I admitted.

"It isn't that difficult, Miss Jamie," he told me matter-of-factly.

"Fine," I thought and thought, then settled on

something. "Once upon a time, there was a lady named Janet who could see ghosts."

Yes, surely ghosts would interest a five-year-old.

"She could see the ghosts, but nobody else could. She was afraid of them. But, one day, she met a man named Edward who taught her that there was nothing to be afraid of."

I paused, searching for something to add, and was shocked to find that Henry had already fallen asleep. I sat up and called his name softly just to make sure that he really was asleep, and stood, pausing in the doorway.

"Eleanor taught *me* not to be afraid," I whispered. I knew that nobody could hear me. It was a good thing. I would certainly be fired if anybody did hear me. "She helped me to not see them anymore at all."

He did not stir, and I left the room and walked down the hall to stand in front of Ruby's closed bedroom door, where I could hear Eleanor reading to her in a hushed voice. I smiled softly and rested my forehead against the door.

"If I ever did see them, she would cover my eyes."

## ACKNOWLEDGEMENTS

Wow! What a journey! I wrote the first draft of this book at seventeen, and at the time, it was a huge source of comfort for me during a time when everything in my life felt incredibly uncertain. This book has grown with me, and it has gone beyond what I ever could have possibly imagined when I first sat down to write it three years ago. I have so many people to thank for this, who I absolutely could not have done this without.

Firstly, of course, thank you to the wonderful people at Engen Books for believing in me and my story, and for helping to make my biggest dreams a possibility. I cannot even begin to express how grateful I am to have worked with you on this project.

Thank you to my family, for constantly supporting my dreams. A special thanks to my mom, my dad, my grandfather, my grandmother, and my siblings, and to Nanny and Poppy Barrett, who I know are cheering me on. I love you all so, so much, and I'm so grateful for you.

Thank you to all of the teachers who have shaped me and encouraged me to keep writing. Most of all, thank you to Ms. Taylor and Ms. Rose, who believed in me throughout the whole process of writing this book, and whose ambition and passion I admire every day. Thank you all!

The biggest thanks to all of my friends, and especially to Vince, Abby, Jesse, Sam, and Maggie, who put up with my ramblings and who have been by my side since the very beginning. You all continue to inspire me every single day. I'm sending you all the biggest hugs, and the most thanks in the world!

Finally, thank you to you, the readers, for your interest in this story! When I began writing this book, I was nervous, as there was very little demand for historical sapphic YA books, especially here in Newfoundland. You have made my biggest dreams come true. I want to remind you that you, too, have the power to make your dreams come true.

I can never truly express how grateful I am for

all of you, and for your support. Until next time, I thank you all for everything. This little book means the world to me, and I really do hope that in some way, it can provide even an ounce of solace for you, as it did for me.

Love,
Taylor

## ABOUT THE AUTHOR

**Taylor Barrett** is an award-winning writer and English student at Memorial University of Newfoundland, who currently lives in St. John's with her family and cat.

A writer from a young age, Taylor works primarily in the romance and thriller genres, and usually focuses on the experiences of queer characters with tight-knit friend groups, or stories about mental health.

Her short story *Family Affairs* was featured in the anthology *Terror Nova: The Thirteenth Exhibit*.

In 2023 her debut novel, *Cover My Eyes*, won the best-prepared pitch award in the 2023 Writers NL Pitch the Publisher awards.

Her stated goal is to spread hope and joy through sharing her writing.